# DIRTY HEADS
## AARON DRIES

© 2021 Aaron Dries

Cover art by Thon

Cover design and interior layout by Scott Cole

Black T-Shirt Books Logo by Chris Enterline

ISBN: 978-0-9994519-8-4

"We are made up of what we've been through and what lies ahead. How we react, reacted, and will someday react. We carve each wrinkle and every bulge or bone. Some self-made Prometheus. Beautifully hideous and horrifically gorgeous. Gods, actually. Sage and stony. Often stupid."

— John Boden, *Jedi Summer with the Magnetic Kid*

FOR BEST
PICTURE QUALITY
PLEASE ADJUST THE
TRACKING CONTROL
ON YOUR VCR

# TWENTY

When you're on the run, when you're marked, you've burned energy you never had so eat everything you can find. Rip that plastic bag open and shovel out the cabbage leaves, flicking off maggots, remembering to sift for broken glass. Don't think about who you used to be, not when you're on your knees in the rain, alley-eating behind a small-town Chinese restaurant. The days of greens before ice cream are dead. Keep your engine full. Because the shadow with too many teeth *wants* you tired. You're easier to catch when you're tired.

A noise in the dark. I spin around, noodle threads dangling from my fingers.

Peer with my good eye.

"Who's there?"

More likely than not it's one of us. They call us The Homeless. It's easier for people to think of us as a mass, a horde, than someone's kid. Even if I'm right, I've spent too many nights sleeping rough under the stars these past two summers to assume the best of others. The quiet turns people street mean. We become insects fighting for rot and shelter. No mercy. No middle ground. I've seen things no nineteen-year-old should. Still, I'd take any one of those sad sons or daughters, with their hunger and underpass confessions they share around tin barrel fires, over the monster.

Maybe I'm being too harsh. Maybe we *always* were insects.

Ants with cosmic universes inside them, going about their business in their ecosystems, bucking against the chain of command, only to learn everything falls apart if they buck too hard. The bully is nothing without the bullied, so the bullied must submit. Teachers need students. Churches without believers are just buildings with pretty windows. Eat. Survive. Parasites turning on parasites because everyone, every last one of us, has a part to play. And we all must feed in the end.

"I said who's fucking there?"

The alley is a throat of shadow ringed with pink and blue neon from the loading dock signs. A curtain of rainwater between me and whoever—whatever—is back there. Looking at me, bone wet, on my knees, next to the Schwinn.

My heartbeat quickens. Thudding blood through my system makes my head feel like it's going to explode. Fear helps you see better in the dark. A shadow moves against the wall. The slop of a foot. Sick decay on the breeze.

Tossing the noodle threads, I fumble for my waterlogged backpack and swing it over my shoulders, the extra weight making my muscles grind. I push my bike into the storm, the front wheel popping on a broken beer bottle. Looking back is never a good idea.

The storm clears. I lean against a tree in a nearby park, too wired to sleep. Country dark is thick with memories that tongue you until you're raw. Light spills across the sky, explosions of sound. Birds caw. Dogs howl. It's still a few days to New Year's Eve, the year 2000, but people are celebrating early. Good for them. I can't help wondering how they'll react if the Millennium Bug, the Y2K we've heard so much about, throws the world into darkness after all. Perhaps, for once, others will experience the panic I live with every day, that uncertainty about starting over. It's like we'll almost be equals.

---

Mannequins in Hawaiian shirts study me, security cameras scanning overhead.

My hands quiver as I reach for the bicycle puncture kit. There's an obvious mall cop to my left, moon face with a mouth like a slit wrist, a tight polo shirt tucked into trousers. I can see his belly button through the fabric. He has an outie.

Tattered sneakers squeak over linoleum as I about-turn with the kit under my arm. Walking is hard when all you want to do is run. I give a sideways look at the fitting rooms where mirrors reveal the man lumbering close behind, Bigfoot in khakis and too-white Reeboks. Can he hear my heartbeat? Is *he* radioing in on it, too?

The exit is ahead with the rest of the mall beyond. Shops are overcrowded with Y2K panic buyers. Detectors will beep when I pass through those doors, and I'll have become a thief again. The boy I used to be would by scared of the person I'd become. We were warned in school about taking drugs, how one pill or puff could knock you down the slippery slope to crime. If only it had been that benign with me. My story doesn't matter. We're all the same to people like the mall cop. Losers who must have brought this on ourselves.

*PING! PING! PING!*

"Stop there!" came the voice. He's fast but I'm faster. "Get—back—here, kid."

His need for oxygen is my ally.

I skid to a stop, the mall cop swinging at me. Arms zoom overhead as I bounce—nimble rabbit—for the emergency exit door, evading doomsday shoppers with their toilet paper and bags of canned fruit. Thump the banister handle and the metal swings inwards. Concrete Jenga stairs leading up and down. Unlike the people in the horror movies I used to love (or imagined I'd watched), I descended. Up was almost always a trap.

"You're in—trouble—now," he yells, voice ricocheting off the walls, trouble-trouble everywhere. Another door reveals itself, and not caring where it leads, I elbow it open and stumble into a piss-smelling indoor carpark where the ceiling is low, halogen lamps bleaching the ground in ovals of light. Run. Dark, light. Dark, light. The thump of the door behind me. Moon-face bigfoot is slowing. Good. I duck under the boom gate, almost losing the puncture kit in the process, and escape.

"Beat you!" I shout back at him. "Beat you, shit for brains!"
I don't think he heard me over the rain.

---

I should've known better than to leave my Schwinn in a reservoir. It's been two years since I ran away, and I'm yet to master cloud-reading the way some do tea leaves. A movie image springs to mind: the psychic bent over her mug, warning teens about werewolves and curses and vampires. But silver does werewolves in. Curses can be broken. Grab some garlic and Dracula gives up the ghost—if you're lucky.

Things weren't that easy in the movie of my life. When I close my eyes, I see the VHS cover of that movie on the shelf at Top Video Universe in Kellyville.

*There's a thirteen-year-old boy on his bike being chased by a silhouette. Creamy* Close Encounters *storm clouds overhead like smoke photographed in water. The kid on the bike resembles me six years ago, face rendered in paint, betraying the film's straight-to-video shoddiness. I pick the tape off the shelf, crack open the clamshell, plastic crinkling under my grip, revealing a cassette someone like the person I used to be forgot to rewind.*

I often think of Top Video Universe and the hours spent there.

Rainwater swishes around my ankles as I climb into the reservoir to pull out my bike and backpack, which snagged on a branch that tumbled off one of the trees. If I'd returned a few minutes later, my whole world may have been washed away.

*Idiot. Mum would spiflicate me for that.*

Shivering, I set to patching my tyre in a nearby underpass. Cars whizz past, coating me in gutter sludge. Make a break for it when the rain eases, bike rolling smooth. Summer sun comes out and I steam as I ride, keeping to the backstreets.

The worst thing about being on the road are the quiet hours when there are no distractions. When you don't think of yourself as a thief any more. You think only of the things stolen from you. *Dee's teases. Mum's side-eye. Aunt Kat and the chocolates she brought when visiting us*. There's only the one-note lullaby of rubber tyre over tarmac now, turning, turning, year after year, leading me away from where everything went wrong, and looping me (maybe without me noticing) back to where it all began.

———————————————————————————————

"Kid's lived," they whisper when my back is turned, when they think I can't hear them.

"Yeah, he's seen some rough stuff."

It's infuriating how people can read the hurt in me at a distance, tracing the rise and fall of my scars with eyes that won't meet my own. Calling these people out—the service workers, parents of kids who usher their families to the other side of the street ("look at his face, Dad!")—for the cowards they are does no good. Learned *that* the hard way. Do that, they'll say you're nuts. You'd have to be nuts to be homeless, right? All that wasted potential! Anger gets the better of me sometimes. Best to push on. Keep my head low. Do what the rubberneckers can't and mind my business.

My travel pack is full of food and medical supplies gathered from community service depots—despite depleted stocks. New Year uncertainty, see. The humiliation of asking for help is something I don't experience any more. I walk into those buildings and clock toys kids outgrew and see something of myself in them. Busted teddy bears awaiting new owners. "Need a place to stay tonight?" said the woman behind the counter at a Salvation Army store two towns back as she loaded up my pack with cans of mystery vegetables. "I could call someone, maybe."

This isn't like being in the cities where there's an organisation or charity. Out here in the Hunter Valley, it's only ever 'someone'. My head dropped.

"I shouldn't be doing this," she said, and opened her purse.

Homeless people are like ghosts that people walk through. I'd forgotten how it felt to be seen. Being given money without having to coerce it or being demanded sex in return made me feel human. The Salvation Army badge pinned to her shirt read 'Marge'. She gave me $250 in cash and saw me struggling to say thank you and told me not to say a thing. Marge turned her back on me, so I didn't have to turn my back on her. A gift of another kind.

Weeping, I set off on my bike into peak Australian summer. Blue jeans sky and flat, rusty countryside pimpled with cattle and bony sheep. Vehicles didn't slow as they passed, fanning dirt and pebbles blasting my skin, which doesn't burn any more. It only hardens.

Townsend Heights—the place I grew up in and haven't been back to since everything happened—revealed itself. Buildings sprawled at a prairie crossroads, seemingly tossed and left there like a giant game of knucklebones. Tin roofs and agriculture trucks and church peaks. Solid, dusty Catholic country.

*Here we go.*

I rode into a park on the other side of the **WELCOME** sign, stepping into the shade of a public toilet by the old War Memorial Pool. There was a man in the far stall rubbing the stubby cock poking through his fly. His wedding ring caught the grubby light as he gestured with his chin for me to come over. He didn't kiss me with his soft married mouth. Whatever. The illusion of not being alone in this world lasted until cum splashed the concrete floor, and then he scuttled off, asking me not to follow him. Like I *would* have.

Outside, I unchained my bike and glanced around. The park was manicured. Families ate picnics. I'm sure from where they were, at that distance, I looked like any other teenager. Not the nineteen-year-old fag with the scarred face you only tolerate when your cock is in my hand. Sailing Frisbees. Sparrows on a power line. The hum of electricity made the headache that was with me most of the time stir again.

I saw my monster.

It stood between bottlebrush trees about a hundred yards away. Bees swarmed about it, wings catching the sun and glowing like embers thrown from a burning mattress under a bridge. My throat dried up. Nobody else in the park noticed this stranger. Was my imagination playing tricks again? It wouldn't be the first time. After all, I might still have a home were it not for my imagination. No, this was real. There must have been a sewer nearby, a manhole or something. My monster moved fastest in the sewers.

Frisbees kept sailing through the air. Families kept laughing. Those birds on the power line didn't fly away. Electricity hummed on, always there, always with me. Like the fear-headache. I got the hell out of there.

---

Houses thin out, a signal I'm close. Better to keep to the outskirts. I've seen enough to know Townsend Heights is a different place now. New traffic lights. Another restaurant. The trees are taller, but everything else has shrunk.

*What happened to all the* LOST CAT *posters we put up back then?*

Towns are corpses (and you see more than you'd like to on the road). Without the spirit of what made them great or worth hating, they end up husks waiting for magic to re-animate them. I can't be the one to bring this place back to life. I've got my own fights to win. I ride the pedals, inertia easing me down a winding dirt road.

*Maybe coming back was a mistake.*

Rubber tread wheels over pebbles. Cicadas sing from eucalyptus trees. It's like I'm in two places at once, going to The Truck Graveyard as a nineteen-year-old with his entire life strapped to his back, and at the same time, as a thirteen-year-old with his sister and friends by his side that Saturday afternoon in 1994. The day it began. It was hot then, too. "Kindling weather," Mum said. "So don't forget your sunscreen. Slip-slop-slap."

I skid to a stop, let the bike fall, ease off the backpack. Sneakers crunch-crunch-crunch over gravel. This place is dense with memory. There's a wire fence with a sign that never used to be there, though.

## WARNING. PRIVATE PROPERTY. DO NOT ENTER.

My fingers curl through the mesh. If I squint, I can almost see Lincoln and I through in the heatwaves wafting off the ancient vehicles, the two of us in our matching black *Jurassic Park* shirts, swarmed by flies. Dee's there, too. She looks unimpressed. I'm shouting warnings at us all.

# NINETEEN

"Holy shit-balls, Batman," said Lincoln Leoung, my best friend. He slapped his thighs, a sound that echoed through The Truck Graveyard like one of the firecrackers his father brought back from Canberra for us. "This is choice-as."

My fingertips stuck to the pages of the old magazine. Glossy girls and guys peeled away with an audible tack. None of us had ever seen anything like this before.

"You got to promise not to tell," I said to Dee.

My younger sister sat across from us, cupping her freckled cheeks. "I said I wouldn't, so I won't." Dee was nine, the age (I'd noted a few years earlier) when you figure the dividends of maintaining a secret, even an itty-bitty one, the way it can be fostered like a wounded bird. Dee had *that* glimmer in her eye. Cheeky, tomboyish, riddled with hints of intelligence, more adult than me in ways that were threatening. I trusted her, even if she had us over a barrel. "But it's rude," she said, crossing her arms, younger than us but showing who was boss, today's compliance cementing tomorrow's briberies.

We'd been playing where we shouldn't have been playing, conspirators and each others' alibi, and in the process discovered something we had no right discovering. The magazine. *SWANKSTERS*, its pages faded and leaf-crisped by the sun, had been on the floor of one of the abandoned cement trucks in Flannigan's Lot, AKA, The Truck Graveyard, end of the line for the lifeline of our shitty town in that corner of New South Wales. I was the one who found it among the cobwebs and beer caps.

Lincoln, who was born in Hong Kong and immigrated to Australia with his family at three, snatched the magazine from my hands. "Who do you think left it?" He crouched by my side, using an elbow to adjust the fanny-pack he'd not long ago unzipped to show off Warheads that changed the colour of your tongue, Pogs for trade, and two envy-inducing Tamagotchis. Mum said Tamagotchis were a waste of money. "You and your sister have got Penny, a real cat, to look after!" We complained anyway. All our worth was measured in what we didn't have, not in what we had.

"One of the drivers," I said to Lincoln, squinting at the field of chrome and broken glass, busted wheels clotted with gummy spider nests. Mum would tan our hides if she knew we were here. Dad, pushover that he was, might show mercy.

"There are articles as well," Lincoln said. "What do you—"

I ripped the porno (even the word felt dirty) back. "Who cares about the articles?"

Dee sighed. "Can we go now? There might be snakes."

"Oh, there's snakes here," I said. "Just because we haven't seen them doesn't mean they haven't seen us." This was something Dad would say, and it felt good in my throat, that flicker of hypocrisy. Something warm and cold at once. Dee backed down.

"What you reckon, Spoons?"

Spoons—Lincoln's nickname for me, short for Spooner. I don't think he ever called me Heath, which was A-OK by me. Guys like resident class bully Brett Oldfield decreed 'Heath' a faggy name. And when you're a thirteen-year-old in Townsville Heights, it paid to listen to guys like Brett Oldfield. Especially if you were the 'target-on-your-back' kind.

"Spoons?"

"Huh?" I said, snapping to.

"Do we take it with us?"

I shook my head. "My parents will spifflicate me if they find this magazine in my room. How about you hold onto it for us?"

"'Spiflicate', dude? Really?" Lincoln said. "Who even says that? Look, I don't know. Mama makes my bed. What if she found it?"

"Or you could, like, make your own bed?"

Dee stood, brushing grit off her overalls—as to how you could wear them on a day that hot was beyond me. It was as though she were grafted to them, inseparable all year round. "I'm bored as shit." She swiped the air to ward off a black static of flies.

"Don't swear, Dee," I said. "It doesn't make you any cooler."

Lincoln glared my way. I glared at the page. The inscription above the man's dark hair read: **Clayton McManus will do things to her no woman has ever experienced before.**

*What does that even mean?*

Hormonal electricity blitzed through me—like when one of the kids in class described 'that scene' from *Basic Instinct*. Movies made the world a bigger place, one rumoured leg-cross at a time. Lincoln said he knew someone's older brother who had a bootleg, that he'd score it for our next sleepover. We didn't have a VCR, and even if we did, I wouldn't bring that film within spitting distance of our place on Mason Drive. What if this hypothetical video got stuck in our hypothetical video machine and my parents had to dig it out with a screwdriver? Or worse, what if they walked in on us watching it? I'd turn to stone on the spot—easy pickings for one of Mum's spiflications.

Clayton who knew how to do things stared up from the crusty page with don't-make-me-hurt-you eyes. Tanned skin (why didn't mine bronze that way?). The sharp jolt of collar bone (crack an egg on it). A chest that didn't look anything like my own (but hopefully would). The tuft of pubic hair (had he trimmed it?). The stupidly sized dick. I wanted to *be* him when I grew up. Screw being a cartoonist. I'd trade every ambition for the paper man's confidence, his promises and power. He stood over the nameless woman, sprawled on her back across green grass, pushing her breasts up at the sky. She didn't seem afraid. And if she was, that fear looked like pleasure.

Adults were weird. Becoming one couldn't come fast enough.

I crab-walked to the hub of the cement truck, and with a sigh, returned Clayton McManus and the naked woman and all their paper girlfriends and paper boyfriends to where we found them, in the hub of the abandoned truck, in a part of Townsend Heights where kids weren't allowed to play. Because it was dangerous, our parents said. There were snakes that saw you even when you didn't see them.

"Buzz-kill Spoons strikes again," Lincoln said.

# EIGHTEEN

*WATCH OUT,* I want to scream at the kids who are no longer there, at myself, the boy whose wish for adulthood would soon come true. Spoons was about to learn how to hate yourself, and about grief. Not that he knew it at the time. How could he know that Saturday was when everything changed, that something strange had caught whiff of him? It still seems impossible that someone as small and insignificant as me could draw the attention of something so powerful, and from so far away. But it did happen. It's *still* happening.

*IT'S COMING! IT'S HERE.*

My younger self doesn't hear me.

The Truck Graveyard is empty. Time to leave. There still might be snakes. I pick up the Schwinn and grip the handlebars to stem the quivering.

*What am I trying to achieve? Do I somehow think I can beat this thing?*

Besides, like the boy I used to be, the places that once meant something to me don't exist. Not how I remembered them, anyway. Nostalgia is a bully. Far worse than Brett Oldfield and his knuckles. So, I ride off, thankful for Marge's $250, prepared to treat myself to the luxury of a bed and shower at the Big Rex Inn on Hunter Street until New Year's Day. Lay low. Mind my business. People might remember me. Spoons, they used to call me. They'll whisper, as they always do.

*Kid's lived. Yeah, he's seen some rough shit.*

My face is a mess of meat. And guilt is my deepest scar.

# SEVENTEEN

"We're going shopping," Mum said the following day after church. "Into town."

Townsend Heights, by definition, was a town. But 'town', as we called it, referred to Kellyville, which was where you went when you required more than over-priced groceries and chicken feed. This news had me fist pumping the air, especially after sweating through one of Father Barnaby's notorious air-sucking sermons. Top Video Universe was next door to the Woolworths my mother (receptionist at a little doctor's surgery where she said the male doctors treated women like dogs) and my father (delivery driver for Saxby's cordial factory) poured their salaries into so we kids could, like the song said, eat well and grow up Happy Little Vegemites. Dee, on the other hand, equated the Kellyville trip to hours of tedium, second only to the church service, her scowl a legendary thing.

We drove with the windows of our Volkswagen Fox rolled down, *Groove Is in the Heart* by World Clique on the radio. Wind blew hair every which way, made roadmaps flutter in door pockets. We had to throw some of them out last time because Dee got car sick and threw up. Everything stunk afterwards and she got to sit in the front seat, as if rewarded. We played I Spy for a while and Dad honked at a fleet of vintage cars dragging tin cans with the words *JUST MARRIED* scrawled across the back windows.

"Did you keep your wedding dress, Mum?" Dee asked.

"It's in my cupboard with all the mothballs," she replied. "I was going to chuck it, but Aunt Kat wouldn't let me. Why you ask? You got your eye on someone?" Mum raised her tone, eyebrow arched as she gave Dad a look.

"Maybeeeee," Dee said. "I'm quite popular, you know." It was the way she pronounced *quite* that made us laugh.

"Oh, are you just?" Mum said. "What about you, Heath?"

"No," I said, wishing Dee had never brought this up. My body tensed, throat thickening. I hated when my parents alluded to me getting a girlfriend. I couldn't even handle being around my family when John Paul Young's *Love is in the Air* came on the radio. It made my stomach knot, knowing at some point they would ask, "Why aren't you singing along with us, Heath?", relishing in how uncomfortable it made me. They weren't being mean. Joshing around was just a part of who we were. But I hated the love stuff and hated it more for not understanding why.

Mum didn't press the matter, focusing on the road ahead instead. From where I sat behind the driver's seat, I could see the neat way she rested her hands on her lap, how sun caught her silver wedding ring. Mum and Dad had each other's names inscribed on the inside of their bands.

*Love.*

I tried to picture myself at the movies in Kellyville, a rose stuffed in my pocket, offering it to a date in the seat beside me at the most romantic part of the film (that's what you did when you liked someone, right?). But who would that person be? Was there anyone in my year who would say yes to going out with me? My mind ping-ponged from girl to girl, and then I half smiled when a lightbulb went off. A dim lightbulb, sure. But a lightbulb. There *might* be someone. However, making a move on her would require bravery I wasn't sure I had. I shifted in my seat, studying the dark hairs on the skinny legs poking out of my shorts, knees criss-crossed with Band Aids from crawling around The Truck Graveyard. My feet jiggled against the car floor. More than once, report cards over the years made mention of me being the nervous type. *Considerate and talented*, teachers wrote. *But over-anxious*. Oh, well. Surely some things I was allowed to be worried about.

Like would *she* say yes if I dared ask her out?

The landscape slid past the window. I measured distance from home in the duration of *Simpsons* episodes, not time or kilometres. Our trip equated to three back-to-back shows, minus commercials. We'd be in Kellyville for six.

*Grove is in the Heart* gave way to *Treaty* by Yothu Yindi. I hummed along, even though I didn't know what the song meant. A journal danced on my lap as Dad dodged potholes but aimed for roadkill, the car jolting, us giving a yell, intestines exploding across the tarmac. Dad would offer a cheeky 'woohoo, 50 points!' at this. He did this to gross us out. To piss Mum off. It worked.

Dad pulled into the carpark out front of Woolworths, opposite the library. Dee asked if she could run over to the public toilets real quick. Mum told her she could use the ones inside the shops, which were cleaner. Dad mentioned he didn't want to catch us using those dunnies because, "Only poofters in them." When Dad took us to the pub on a Sunday and let me play pool with him and his mates, I often heard them referring to the spider cue, used for guiding shots players couldn't pull off without an aid, the 'poofter stick'. Best I knew, the word meant weak. That toilet by the carpark was used by weak men. Okay, sure.

Doors slid open to offer what we never got at home: air-conditioning. Only, no. That wasn't true. We had an upright fan Mum draped with a wet towel. During kindling weather, that damp air worked wonders, but we complained anyway, which made Mum angry. Like her attempts to make something out of nothing hadn't been good enough.

Regardless, the mall air was magic. Cold and sugary. I'm sure Mum enjoyed it, too.

"Right, you lot," Dad said, hands on hips. He was rake-thin like me. I wonder if school had been hard for him, too. Not that I asked, nor did I reveal how difficult those fourteen or so episodes of *The Simpsons* were for me. We were alike, Dad and I. Bookworms. A bit guarded. Mum said Dad had hair just like me when he was my age, dark and thick and impossible to keep neat. Now his hair was white. His mates called him Snowy. I jiggled my foot against the mall linoleum, jittery again. "You both listening?" Dad said.

"Yes, Dad," we answered in a beginning of class drone.

"Dee, stay by Heath's side. Heath don't let your sister out of your sight. You hear?"

"Yeah."

"Heath?" Serious now. "Look at me when I'm speaking to you."

I did. Obligation met obligation, man to man-to-be. We connected. We understood. "Dee, be sure to listen to your brother. He's in charge until we're done."

"Meet us out front of the store in an hour," Mum said. She always was the serious one, even when happy. "And not a minute after. Don't make me come look for you."

Her voice was stern—but stern because she cared, the voice of someone who didn't suffer fools lightly because foolishness wasted time. Her muscles shifted beneath her floral blouse. I was reminded, then, of framed photographs of Mum by the staircase lining the wallpaper like fat summer flies. These images chronicled Spooner history. Dad often reminded us that we didn't have much in the way of money, that we were a lifetime of hard work and one day of rotten luck from being poor. But our camera—an old Nikon that resembled a Snickers bar you held horizontal to your face with two hands for fear you dropped it—was never without film. Mum's hand was firm, Dad's was prone to shakes. One particular photo captured Mum (younger than I could ever imagine her being) mid-swing, long hair flying, as she lugged an iron shot into the air. Her sister, our beloved Aunt Kat and only relative, was in the corner of the frame, cheering her on. I once asked Mum when and where the picture had been taken.

"That was in high school," she said, her usual sternness slipping for a moment. "I wasn't into cheerleading or gym like the other girls. Shotput was my thing. I've even got a couple of trophies in the basement to prove it, too. Was a long time ago, Heath."

"A shot-*put?*" I'd asked, fiddling with the slap-bracelet on my wrist.

Mum smiled and took me to her bedroom where she sat me on the edge of their mattress. It smelled like her and Dad in here— her cloying perfume, his cheap cologne. I watched Mum shuffle to the tall boy, tiptoeing to rifle through odds-and-ends jigsawed on top. She drew down a wooden box and took her place beside me.

"This is a *shot*, sweetheart."

She drew out one of two metal spheres, each the size of a baseball.

"Wow," I said, cupping it. Enjoying its chill. "It's heavy."

"Sure is."

"Must really take something to lob it good."

"You bet it does, Heath. Bigtime heave-ho."

"Did Aunt Kat play, too?"

"Ha, no. You'd sooner see her on the moon. Her health wasn't so great, even back then."

Mum took the shot from my hand with powerful thin fingers and returned it to the velveteen box. Her smile, too, stowed away among the dust bunnies. I asked Mum if I could take that photo of her out of its frame and keep it in my backpack. She agreed. There were times when I took it out at recess to steal a quick glance, to keep me strong. It helped more than I ever allowed her to know.

*Big time heave-ho…*

"—Heath," Mum said, stern, snapping me back to reality. The mall fluorescents made her split ends look silver. "Are you listening?"

"Yep. We'll meet you here in an hour. No excuses. We won't make you come for us."

"Good. If we're running a smidge over time, sorry but stay put. Roger?"

"Roger that," I said, notebook and pencil case tight in one hand.

"Okay you two," Dad chimed in, smiling. "Off you trot."

So, trot we did—right next door to Top Video Universe.

# SIXTEEN

I AM LIGHTNING SEARCHING THE UNIVERSE FOR SOIL TO STRIKE.

BOILING, CHURNING, I TURN AND GRIND WITH ENERGY SAPPED FROM STARS. THE BLACKNESS THEIR FADING LEAVES BEHIND IS A DELIGHT. EVERY HOUSE I UPEND, EVERY GUN I TRIGGER, CREATES AN ABSENCE TO MOURN. AND I DRINK THAT MOURNING, IMITATE WHAT YOU MIGHT CALL A LAUGH. I DON'T KNOW WHAT LAUGHTER IS. I'M YET TO LEARN THAT. I HOPE TO, EVEN AS I BOIL, AS I CHURN AND GRIND. I AM THE GROUT BETWEEN THE BRICKS. THE MICRO-DREAM BETWEEN ROAD AND ONCOMING TRUCK. THE FRECKLE BEFORE THE SURGERY. THE LOVER WHO FUCKS YOU AND ISN'T AROUND THE MORNING AFTER. I AM THE HOPE YOU LOST. I'M THE ONE YOU NEVER FORGET BUT DON'T TELL HIM, HER, THEM, ABOUT. I'M THE SECRET YOU DON'T WANT ANYONE TO LEARN. I'M THE FANTASY OF THAT SECRET GETTING OUT, THE CHURNING IN YOUR GUTS AT THE THOUGHT—BECAUSE NOBODY CAN BE TRUSTED WITH YOUR TRUTHS, NOT EVEN YOU. I'M THE JESTER WHO POISONED THE KING. THE DRUG YOU THOUGHT WAS SAFE. THE CORD YOU TRIPPED OVER. THE PAPER YOU CUT YOURSELF ON. I AM ASH, THE GAS IN YOUR LUNGS. I'M ME. IT.

YOU. THIS. THAT. I WILL BE. I NEED THIS. I NEED THE EARTH. GUIDE ME. TAKE ME HOME. I KNOW YOU WANT THIS. YOU'VE COME TOO FAR TO TURN BACK. I HAVE YOUR ARTERIES—TUG, TUG. AND I KNOW WHY YOU WANT TO HELP ME. YOU WANT TO WATCH IT BURN. KINDLING WEATHER. TAKE ME TO GROUND.

# FIFTEEN

Dee went to the corner of Top Video Universe by the big windows overlooking the street. That's where she normally hung out, a silhouette with other kids around a table with crayons. There was almost always a parent hovering about, browsing the Coming Soon catalogues. Not that day, though. Dee amused herself alone. It was unusually quiet.

*Good. No distractions.*

My heart raced. *Walk fast as you can, but don't run. Don't appear too eager—that ain't cool.* Aisles glided by, passing square-jawed cardboard action heroes toting guns, a grim reaper with flashing bulbs for eyes, and posters on the walls, floating heads pouting and hungry for revenge, because, yeah, this time it *was* personal. The two clerks behind the counter knew me by name and I loved that. Not the icky love I'd been nudged by in the car ride over, not John Paul Young love. This was high-five love between people on the level.

"Heath, my man," said Stacy with the nose-ring. "Where's the fire?"

"Hi," I called over my shoulder. Waved. Kept running. "Bye!"

"Catch you, little dude," said Brennan with the blue hair before turning to load a line of video cleaners into the machines, the tangy scent of alcohol in the air as deck heads whirred dirt accumulated in renter's homes off the tapes.

If I couldn't be a cartoonist when I grew up, carving out a career as a full-time video store clerk sounded sweet. Just so long as I resembled Clayton McManus, only maybe with a colour in my hair, a nose ring, all of it a contract binding me to late returns I'd happily chase, fishing tapes from buckets under the slot in the wall.

*Wow,* I thought. *All the wows in the Milk Way.*

My Chuck Taylor's skidded over smelly acrylic carpet, building static electricity to guarantee a zap later. I didn't care. I was here. Here and charged. The banner suspended from the ceiling in the far left-hand corner read **HORROR**.

VHS clamshells lined the aisles, most covers facing outwards, some spines first. Plastic caught the light, every rainbow shade on show in the white-lie marketing. *Be Kind, Rewind* stickers everywhere. My admiration made everything that didn't involve this place pale. Top Video Universe was the only schoolyard that mattered.

*Here, I'm the Grand Goomba.*

I started at A, as always. Taking your time was part of the fun, a tease I indulged because midway through that section, anticipation for Bs cranked into gear. It didn't matter that I'd been to this store a hundred times or more, that the inventory expanded in intermittent lurches. The thrill never dimmed. I just had to pace things right so I wouldn't be forced to speed through T to Z as our deadline closed in. Every minute counted.

"How's it hanging, Heath?" asked Stacy with the nose ring. "Your parents shopping up a storm next door?"

"Sure are," I replied from where I sat cross-legged in the D section, notepad splayed across my knees. The ballpoint pen scratched, scratched.

"Buddy, that's pretty damn sick!" I glanced up at Stacy who peered down at my drawing from over the tape stack in her arms. "That's the *Deep Star Six* cover?" she said.

"Yup."

"You're talented, buddy."

Complements on my art—not that I really considered it as

such (though I viewed what I plagiarised as significant as the Mona Lisa we'd studied in class)—made me uncomfortable in a good way. At Top Video Universe, lightyears from St Bridget's, I allowed myself a dirty self-confidence that could only exist within these walls, under those lights, in front of peers who mattered. Part of that confidence involved ignoring the compliment itself.

Stacy stepped into the boxed-off section in the corner where kids weren't allowed. A beaded curtain separated here from there. I wasn't naïve as I looked, knew what was inside. *Clayton and all his porno girlfriends.* The store remained empty except for us that day, but there had been times when it was full of men who dared slide through those curtains. They would glance about, wearing trucker hats, stomachs bulging over their jeans. Whenever those plastic beads sang, you couldn't help noticing. I never caught much of a view of the Adult Corner's interior—a peep of flesh. I wondered if I'd have the confidence to be like those men and just stroll on in when I was old enough, lay those videos down on the counter. Would Stacy or Brennan judge me, knowing I took those videos home to beat off to? How could they *not* judge me? Did Stacy and Brennan watch that kind of stuff? Wait—did my parents?

*Stop thinking.* My neck flushed. *Take a breath.*

Sighing, I slotted *Deep Star Six* with its mutilated diver on the cover into its place on the shelf and shuffled along. So many movies. Some familiar, others not. *Deadly Friend.* Scanned and put it back, sketching in my notebook as I went. The E section called—shrieked. F after that, another siren. Tick-tock, tick-tock. *From a Whisper to a Scream*: the severed head making my skin prickle. *Lifeforce* with its naked woman strapped to a tubular pod in outer space. My fingertips accumulated dust as I went. *The Mutilator*, featuring a row of scantily clad teenagers who didn't resemble anyone at my school cowering before a meat hook. *Puppet Master 3* (the main puppet had six arms!). *Sleepwalkers* and all its cats approaching a house set against a purple sky—that one I'd seen.

Lincoln and I had been at a friend's place for an overnight birthday party where we were (more or less) left to our own devices. Popcorn buttered and brought into the garage in Tupperware bowls.

Pillows thrown. No girls allowed. Someone loaded up the VCR once his parents turned in, our friend giving us a mischievous wink. The tracking feature battled tape haze. Dirty heads. He ran a cleaner through the machine and tried again. Success. "Just wait 'til you see this," he proclaimed. "The dude fucks his mother and then they turn into cats. Plus, someone gets stabbed to death with a corn cob!" Lincoln and I re-enacted that scene for weeks. My appetite for the weird stuff cemented—not that it was easy to come by. The drawings I spent hours on afterwards, riddled with speech bubbles full of exclamation marks, depicted more and more dead bodies. Wounds. All the wounds in the Milky Way.

I moved through the aisle.

Ghouls. Faces in distress. Knives dripping blood. Women who covered their faces to expose armpits, suggestions of breasts in shadows as something chased them through the trees. What, though? That was what kept me coming back again to pick up what these VHS covers threw down. The *what?* Why was less important. Speculation echoed in my head, in sketches on the page. Good sketches, according to Stacy with the nose ring. Imagining what stories played out beyond the titles was the only option open to me. Because I couldn't borrow a single video.

This had nothing to do with most of the films being R-rated.

Top Video Universe was geo-blocked to those in the Kellyville area. We lived multiple *Simpsons* episodes away, down a road paved with roadkill, in a duplex on Mason Drive in Townsend Heights. It didn't matter that Stacy and Brennan with the blue hair knew me by name or that they complemented my work. The store—my first real love—had gatekeepers. And like first love, as I'd soon find out, this one, too, was unrequited.

"Heath?"

The pencil in my hand stopped moving, those dark eyes unfinished for now. I faced my sister. She didn't have to tell me it was time to leave. I already knew.

# FOURTEEN

FEEL IT? HAIRS RISING. A RUSH OF BLOOD YOU'D SOONER
DENY THAN ENJOY. BECAUSE YES, YOU ARE GOING TO TAKE
ME. I'M NEITHER THE BULLET NOR THE GUN. I'M THE TARGET
YOU NEVER KNEW YOU WANTED TO BRING HOME. YOU'VE
COME THIS FAR. NOW SHOW ME MORE.

I KNOW YOU WANT TO. I CAN FEEL YOUR HAIRS RISING—
LAUGHTER TO ME. I CAN FEEL THE BLOOD PUMPING INTO
YOUR COCK, YOUR CLITORIS, SWELLING, TINGLING. THERE,
RIGHT THERE. THAT'S ME. I'M (WE ARE) IN YOU. AND YOU'RE
SHOWING ME (US) WHERE TO EARTH. CLOUDS TURNING, FOG
THAT CLOTS UNTIL THOUSANDS CHOKE. I'M THE FANTASY
THAT REMAINED A FANTASY UNTIL THE MOMENT IT WASN'T.
SO, SHOW ME. DO IT. FOR ONCE IN YOUR LIFE BE MORE THAN
THIS AND SMILE. GRAB ME. SHAKE ME. RIP ME OPEN WITH
YOU. PUSH ME DOWN, DOWN, DOWN, DOWN THERE. I KNOW
YOU'RE READY TO EVOLVE. LET ME HELP YOU DO THAT. AND
REMEMBER THE NUMBER 2 AND THE 4 AND THE 8.

YOU'RE SAYING YES. YOU'RE SMILING. LET ME IN.

# THIRTEEN

Dee was the first to bound out of the car once we were home—only to be called back to help carry groceries. The way she slouched and stomped was predictable and annoying. Sometimes the weight of the cans pinched the bag handles so tight the tips of my fingers turned blue. One day, the plastic gave way and a pumpkin dropped on my toe. I'd screamed. Dee laughed. Later, my nail went black and had to be removed by a doctor in Kellyville. I assimilated this memory into one of my drawings. Morbid, Mum called it.

Our duplex shared a wall with 6B Mason Drive, which hadn't been rented in six months. Townsend Heights was a place people left, not moved to. Our landlords—a couple who joined us for dinner sometimes and liked to drink wine that made their teeth blacken—owned both properties. I liked them. "They're mad as cut snakes," Dad would say.

We trudged everything inside, helped put it all away. Our tabby, Penny, meowed from the kitchen corner, waiting for her bowl to be filled. Dad went to his study to read. The walls of that office were covered in fantasy books that smelled of dusty nothings. Cobwebs latticed the window. There were hardcovers on the top shelf I wasn't allowed to read. Dad said I could crack them open when I was old enough, a promise I planned to hold him to.

Two years earlier, one of the guys in class passed around a tattered copy of *Carrie* he'd swiped from his mother and let me photocopy parts on our lunchbreak. I read these excerpts in bed by torchlight and threw them away afterwards, worried my parents would stumble across them. Those pages introduced me to many things, including menstruation. To say I was confused would be an understatement.

"Take this downstairs, please." Mum handed me a box of laundry detergent. "Pop it next to the washing machine."

"Okay, okay, I know where it goes." Summer days were long. Time enough to squeeze in quality play before dinner—assuming chores didn't absorb the remaining hours. No wonder I was antsy. Mum side-eyed me. I apologised and clip-clopped into the basement, Penny at my heels. Shelves grinned under the weight of paint cans and toolboxes. A bulb on a wire illuminated the space, moths throwing huge shadows over the walls.

Mum used to scold me for spending so much time down here. Her sternness lost its edge once she saw what I was up to. I would unroll a blanket on the oil-splattered concrete and draw for hours on end. "At least it's keeping you out of trouble. But you really should be outside more. Do you want us to buy you a football, or something?"

Ha.

I knew I'd end up in the humid basement after dinner, continuing my VHS stories in 2HB pencil, page after page. Sometimes, I mumbled dialogue under my breath as I imagined the killer's motive. Even though it was scarier when you didn't know *why* they did it.

Penny meowed as I put the detergent in its rightful place. Dee pranced by the lawn-level window mounted into the wall. *She's got the right idea*, I thought, and then I escaped the house to ride over to Lincoln's place.

"Helmet please," Mum called from the front door. I laid down my second-hand BMX and sprinted to my room on the second floor at the end of the hall, muttering about rules and how much they sucked.

My bed was made. Movie posters I'd bought from Top Video

Universe for fifty cents glared from the walls. Sometimes the Blu-Tack lost its stickiness, poster corners peeling free in the middle of the night. The following morning, I would stand on my mattress and force them back into place. I wasn't allowed to use tape on the blue wallpaper that had been there for as long as I could remember (the wallpaper in Dee's room was pink).

More rules. More whatevers.

The Leoungs lived in a big house that smelled different from ours. Sneeze-gifting spices. Piles of flip-flops in plastic. Boxes with funny postage marks. Too many clocks. Mrs Leoung always offered me Diet Coke in a recyclable bottle with a curly straw. Mum didn't like me badgering on about how much I enjoyed visiting them and the fancy things they had. "Mister Leoung gave me something called a mooncake, and it was nice and weird, and—"

"If you like it so much you can go live there," Mum snapped one time from where she'd been stirring spaghetti bolognaise on the stove, a Spooner staple she made rich and soupy. Delicious. We weren't allowed to wear white when we ate it.

Lincoln and I stripped down to our Underoos and jumped in his pool. His mother called to him, and he answered in Chinese.

"It's insane that you can speak two languages, dude," I said.

"White people, I tell you."

"Fuck you, dick-smear." I tossed a boogie board at him. He launched it back.

My best friend shot a nose-full of snot into the pool. "We should go back for that magazine."

"Gross. And no. Too risky. Besides, Dee was right. There are snakes there."

"Is there anything that *doesn't* scare you, Spoons?"

"And you're, like, Mister Bravery."

This was how we talked, a back and forth of trying to out-do and out-play one another. We would rag on those making school hell (namely, *the* Brett Oldfield) and fantasise about what we'd do to him, the booby-traps we'd set to snap his legs or chop off his head. Or we'd talk about the guys we wanted to grow into, all modelled after dudes in movies.

Tina, Lincoln's sister, joined us. She had a magazine under one arm and wore loveheart-shaped sunglasses. Sprinklers leapt from the earth to hose her down, evoking a yelp. Her brother erupted with laughter.

"Shut up, Didi," she said, reclining in one of the sun chairs, ankles crossed. I asked him what the nickname meant once and he reluctantly told me it translated to 'shorty'. "Hi, Heath!" Tina gave me a half smile and then raised the copy of *Teen Drama* to her face. She must have had at least twenty butterfly clips in her hair that day, plastic catching the afternoon light and making her head flame. "Don't drown, boys."

I noticed her sparkle-glossed lips beneath the pages from where I floated, hugging the pool's edge. She wore a cut-off shirt pitched by the curve of her breasts. I promised myself to gift her a mixtape that secretly announced my puppy love. Lincoln need not know. In fact, I was sure he'd flip if he found out.

*The rose I pull from the pocket of my jeans in the dark cinema in Kellyville is for her. Tina who likes butterfly hairclips and is in the ninth grade. She smiles. Accepts the flower. Tells me what I sweetie I am and leans across to kiss me.*

Air brushed me as I rode home, passing houses that never changed, toddlers with Tonka trucks in yards, powerlines sagging under the weight of mynah birds. You knew you were getting closer to my house by the number of cars in the yards, by how long the grass was. The sky rolled purple. An airplane droned by.

I wondered if I'd ever travel someday.

Dee and I did the dishes after dinner, our parents retreating to the living room to watch Mum's programs, Dad cracking open a stubby of beer, laughing with sitcom tracks that never rang true to me. My sister and I didn't speak as we scrubbed bolognaise sauce from the plates, sharing Sunday dread. School tomorrow. Finished, stinking of greasy soap suds, I sat with Mum and Dad for a while. Their sitcom went to commercials, and a familiar public service announcement aired. It sucked oxygen from the room, killing our chatter.

A row of men and women were lowered onto a foggy aisle like pins at an alley, only to be mowed down by the Grim Reaper's bowling ball. A man's voice told us that AIDS wasn't just for gays and drug users but could strike down anyone—parents, fathers, little crying girls with blonde pigtails. And if not stopped, it might destroy more people than the Second World War. Fade to black. A sigh of relief among us. Cut to: Thirty seconds of stop motion vegetables coming alive to sexualised music (*oooohhhh, ahhhhhhh, mmmmmmmm*) and gyrating across a tub of Flora butter.

I took this as my cue to leave and went upstairs to grab my battery-operated cassette/radio player, and journal. My stomach ached as if I'd eaten too many sweets, a sickly rejection of something in my body. It passed, and I shuffled into the basement, drew out the blanket pinched with dried glue splotches and tossed it across the concrete. Penny, who had followed me into the stuffy room, nuzzled against my Band-Aided kneecaps. I cupped her face, trying to dull images of Grim Reapers with bowling balls. The memory throbbed. An infection. It struck me weird that I could study horrific VHS covers and watch violent movies, but that advertisement, with its hooded skull face and the cracking sound effect of Australians being struck down, terrified me.

Every now and then something scurried under the shelves. I flinched. Mum had laid out traps the week before—I could see one by the washing machine, the cheese going green. I felt rat eyes on me as I sketched. Penny slinked towards the darkened corner.

"Hear something, girl?" My voice was a whisper.

Bored, the cat returned to my side to bathe. Her continuous purring was an engine of affection you had to earn. It comforted me. The infected throb eased, faded.

I drew in my journal, embellishing what I'd started at Top Video Universe: *The Slaughtering's* front cover. But making it more my own. If I was being objective, the Stacy with the nose rings of the world might say it was better than the actual monster on the VHS, even in this black and white form, without all the fancy fonts and stickers.

My version of the creature was mid-lurch, bald head poised so its eyes bored into you. Muscle and bones warped bruised skin, as though the monster—humanoid in many ways—had been wrung out like a towel, innards reshaping within the tightness of that pull. A Barbie doll crotch between legs of different size. So, it would limp. Thumping when it chased you down. Lips tilted sideways from chin to ear, lacking a nose to set the geometry right. Blisters divided skin from gums and a knot of teeth. This was a creature born to force the pain it felt in its body on other people, the innocents in the movie. *I hurt*, you could almost hear The Slaughterer say. *And that's why you will hurt, too.* I chewed the pencil, deliberating. Should I? Yes. Buffered the paper, shavings backhanded onto the floor. Glanced around to make sure nobody was looking. Sketched in an erect, oversized penis. A familiar tingle in my middle, the sensation of having done something I shouldn't have.

I set the drawing aside and pulled the radio to my knees, startling Penny. "Sorry, girl." I tuned the frequency to 93.5FM. If it sounded overproduced and sugary enough to give you an auditory cavity, those were the songs for me. A chorus of boyband *woos* stained the air. I crunched the PAUSE and RECORD buttons, peered through the Perspex deck to ensure the sprockets were turning. It annoyed me when the announcer cut into the song early. I hit PAUSE and waited for the next tune to come along, one worthy of Tina. I sang along as I sketched, scared but excited by the prospect of giving this to her tomorrow.

Penny glanced around.

More scratching.

The noise was easy to ignore, so long as I kept busy. Record, hold, record. I realised that you made mixtapes for others, but deep down, you just made them for yourself.

*I love this and you will too. Be like me. Tell me you dig me.*

Scratching. Scratching. Scratching.

Done, I gathered up my stuff and stashed the blanket. Penny heard the rustling again. Louder this time. It came from behind the paint cans, I'm sure. She gave a hiss, loud and sharp. My skin pebbled, hairs raising.

What if the rat was rabid (something I always worried about from what I'd learned studying the VHS of *Cujo* hundreds of times, only to have my mother remind me again that there wasn't rabies in

Australia)? What if the rat bit me? Or what if it wasn't a rat at all, but an alien that had crashed to Earth and crawled into our basement to get away from the government, men in black who made kids forget things if they learned too much?

Penny slinked upstairs, paws pat-pat-patting.

My heartbeat returned to its normal speed, and I reached to pull the drawstring light, steeling myself against the oncoming black. Shaking fingers tightened the tab. Pulled.

Click.

The scratching issued again. Lincoln would laugh at me for being such a chicken. *It's nothing. Rats eat and shit and then die after a summer or two. Big whoop.* Jaws grinding, teeth clacking, I left the vermin (or potential alien) to the dark.

After taking a whizz upstairs, I studied my reflection in the bathroom mirror. Pulled faces. Checked my underarms for hair. No developments. Patience was a virtue, or so Mum said when she saw me aching.

Something *clapped*. I glanced down the hall, breath held. A car screeched outside, light swirling through the living room blinds. It was just the rat trap going off in the basement, not the Grim Reaper's bowling ball cracking bones of children who could get AIDS like the gays and drug users on the news, and then die. I went to bed, watched over by movie poster people who never blinked. My notepad sat, closed tight with all the drawings inside, on the windowsill. Warm summer air patted the flyscreen. Crickets droned. Fear ebbed for an hour until sleep pushed it back.

# TWELVE

Found you.

# ELEVEN

Tina's mixtape was wrapped in Christmas paper taken from the recycling shelf in the pantry above the winter sheets. Mum never let things go to waste. She'd watch us like a hawk as we peeled paper off our presents that December morning, diving to catch what we dropped, storing wrappings for Christmases to come. We always stirred her about this. Another family joke. But it came in handy now. I shuffled the mixtape into my backpack next to the photograph of my mother—her iron shot raised—and trotted downstairs, dressed for school.

"Don't you go getting cereal all over your shirt, Dee," Mum said, a piece of toast in her mouth. My sister scrunched her face and dug into her breakfast. Dad laced up his steel-capped boots, bent in his chair as I took my place with a thud. 8am edged nearer.

A handheld wireless on the windowsill screeched the weather report—total fire ban, temperatures rising—giving way to Michael Jackson's *Black or White*. I wished they'd played this the night before, so I could've recorded it for Tina. We all sang along, Mum somehow getting the lyrics wrong, dancing around to hand me an apple from the fridge to put in my father's brown paper lunch bag that she'd set on the ironing board.

"Right-e-o, gang," Dad said, stretching his back so the bones cracked. "You all do your best today." That's what he always said before heading off. Like our little jokes, we all had our little sayings. "It's all we can ask of you."

Mum, tying her hair back with a braid, toast replaced by a bobby-pin between her teeth, bounced to her husband to let him plant a kiss on her cheek. "Later, darl'," she said.

"I should be home on time," he said. "All my deliveries are in the neighbourhood."

"Can you cook?"

"I might pick up some lamb chops. Kids, approve?"

We nodded, me giving Dad a thumbs up as I chewed.

*"Be gooooood,"* he said in his best E.T. impersonation, walking backwards into the living room with his index finger raised. Keys clattered. (Going). The clank of the screen door slapping. (Going). His van roared to life, and then faded. (Gone).

"Rinse your dishes, you two," Mum said. "Got all your things? Dee, did you pick up your homework from where you left it on the rug in the lounge room?"

"Yes, Mum."

"Heath, don't forget your hat. Kindling weather today."

"Roger that," I replied in a robot voice.

"Be sure to wear it on your walk to school, please," she said, saying this because she knew I wouldn't unless pressured to. I hated that wide-brimmed bucket hat. It made me look like a dweeb, and on top of that, weirdly young, baby birdish.

"I will," I said, defensive.

"Oh, Mum!" Dee yelled. "Dad's forgot his lunch."

I looked up from my bowl. The brown paper bag still sat on the edge of the ironing board by the door to our yard, a lot of land homing one lonely lemon tree the summer sun had killed. "Catch him before he goes," Mum said.

Dee bounced across the room, snatched the bag and made a run for it. Funny how she could go from being sluggish to hyperactive so fast. She shuffled back into the room, slinked into her seat to tell everyone what I already knew. "Missed him, sorry."

Mum emptied a can of cat food into a bowl for Penny.

Meows gave way to chewing, wet slops. Brown paper crunched under my mother's grip as she returned Dad's lunch to where Dee found it. "Well, your father's around town all day. He'll come back for it when he's hungry. Okey-dokey, you two. Time to go."

The day greeted us, and we put on our hats. Even me. Though with a certain degree of reluctance. Dee and I trod off in one direction, St Bridget's being a fifteen-minute walk. Mum went the opposite way to catch her bus. I think we left the basement door ajar.

# TEN

I TAKE FORM IN THE MUSTY BASEMENT THAT I STRUCK FROM THE NOWHERE THAT ISN'T THIS PLACE AND TIME. IT IS A GREAT THING TO BE BORN, THE MOMENT YOU ARE ONE THING AND THEN BECOME ANOTHER.

DUST MOTES SWIM. I DRAW THEM IN, AS I DO THE SUNLIGHT THROUGH THE WINDOW. PARTICLES CLOT. ELECTRIC APPLAUSE, CLOUDS CHURNING A STORM. THERE'S A QUIET SPARK AND I AM REMINDED OF THE BURDEN OF WEIGHT.

A STAR OF MEAT ON THE FLOOR. IT'S A CAGE I PUSH OPEN, SPILLING VEINS THAT TRACE UNEVEN GROUND. THIS SPOT IS FERTILE, RICH WITH WANTS. SOMETHING UNSEEN MADE FROM SOMETHING THAT NEVER WAS, A COSMIC PUZZLE COMING TOGETHER, EDGES ALIGNING AND FUSING INTO BONES. AT SOME POINT, I AM CURSED WITH VISION AND ITS LIMITATIONS, THE KIND OF SIGHT THAT ROBS THE UNIVERSE OF ITS MAGIC. SCRAPS OF PAPER FLY THIS WAY AND THAT. THE LIGHTBULB SWAYS SO HARD IT CRACKS AGAINST THE CEILING, RAINING SHARDS THAT BECOME MY TEETH. NAILS SKID ACROSS CONCRETE TO GUILD MY GULLET, SO THAT WHEN I SWALLOW WHAT I NEED, THE REMAINDER OF THEM FEELS

PAIN ALL THE WAY DOWN.

MY ORGASM SPURTS SKIN I CRAWL INTO, AND NERVES FRENZY. PAIN IN EVERY THREAD OF ME AS PURPOSE KNITS ME TOGETHER. SOMETHING CLATTERS, DRAWN INTO MY VORTEX: A DEAD RAT ON A TRAP. WE BECOME ONE. FUR GROWS INWARDS AND SPLITS INTO FOLLICLES THAT PUSH BLOOD THROUGH MY SKELETON. CANS OF PAINT OVERTURN, THEIR CONTENTS SPLITTING INTO A THOUSAND DROPS LIKE PINPOINTS ON A MAP, TURNING, TURNING, AND THEN SUCKED INTO ME AND ABSORBED.

I PUSH UP, PAIN SEARING. THE HEAVINESS IN MY UPPER HALF ARCHES A SPINE THAT I ONLY NOW REALISE HAS A PART TO PLAY IN MY DESIGN. JOINTS SNAP, ENTHUSIASTIC. MY EYES MEET THE CREATURE AT THE FOOT OF THE STAIRS, ITS PELT RAISED, ITS MOUTH OPEN IN A HISS. EVEN IN MY CURRENT STATE, MY HUNGER IS QUICKER THAN ITS RETREAT. I SNATCH THE CAT BY THE TAIL AND YANK IT INTO MY SMILE. IT SLASHES ME AS I CHEW. THE THING IS NOT EATEN. IT IS CONSUMED. A BEAT OF GLUTTONY.

BORN, FATIGUE LEAVES ME SPENT. OXYGEN BALLOONS MY LUNGS, WIND THROUGH A THOUSAND REEDS, STALKS CLATTERING IN A MILLION PARTS OF THIS EARTH AT ONCE. THERE IS A PART OF THEM ALL IN ME, AS THERE IS A PART OF ME IN EVERYTHING. MY KINDRED.

THEY SING!

THIS ROOM, THE BASEMENT, IS EMPTY OF RICHNESS, A HUSK. WARMTH ON MY HIDE FROM THAT LIGHT THROUGH THE WINDOW. HOW DISAPPOINTING IT MUST BE FOR THAT IMMENSE HEAT TO HAVE TRAVELLED SO FAR FROM ITS DYING STAR TO ILLUMINATE A SPACE SUCH AS THIS. NOTHING LASTS FOREVER, NOT EVEN THE SUN. EXCEPT FOR ME. US. SO, BEST TO BURN WELL.

I'M STILL HUNGRY.

# NINE

Students shot from rooms when the lunchtime bell rang, dodging nuns yelling at us to stop running in the hallways. Freedom equating two *Simpsons* episodes beckoned us onto quadrangles and sports fields. Footballs kicked, caught. Guys sneaked hugs from girlfriends under staircases, careful to not get caught by teachers who'd sooner throw a teenager in Principal Dahl's office than let them discover who they were one kiss at a time.

I ate with Lincoln. And was still hungry afterwards.

My best friend droned on about some television show he was obsessed with, *Earth 2*, his words fading into rhythmic underwater mwha-mwahhs. The world rolled black and white as every part of me searched for Tina.

*There she is.*

"Hang tight," I said, snatching up my backpack.

Tina was on her own listening to her Walkman, gliding between demountables in the direction of the chapel. My wide-brimmed hat slid off my head, strap catching my throat as I ran the opposite way, dodging kids playing handball and tag. Like a spy in an old Saturday afternoon movie, I side-stepped into the corridor of the main building. Breaths eluded me, but I pushed on, running straight into all five feet of Brett Oldfield.

Our collision fluffed a cloud of Lynx deodorant. I swear I could taste him in my mouth as I picked myself off the ground. The bully glared at me, incredulous, as if *daring* to share his oxygen—let alone running into him—was the ultimate offence known to kid-kind.

———  —  — · ·  —  —· —· —  ·  —  · ·  ———  ———  ———  —  — · —· ·

MUSCLES FLEX. I USE THESE NEW ARMS TO SHIFT THE WASHING MACHINE AWAY FROM THE WALL. IN DRINKING FROM THE LIGHT AND THE DARK AND THE ENERGY OF THE ROOM, I ABSORB, TOO, THE UNDERSTANDING OF ITS SPACE AND CONTENTS. THIS FEEDING BRINGS WITH IT AN UNDERSTANDING OF SPEECH, DESIGN, AND LIMITATIONS OF THE FLESH. SCRAPING METAL AGAINST CONCRETE MAKES FOLLICLES IN MY EARS REVERBERATE—A SHOCK. STILL, I HEAVE THE MACHINE A FEW INCHES FURTHER, WIDE ENOUGH FOR ME TO SLIDE BEHIND IT. I CAN STRETCH MY BODY IN WAYS HUMAN BREEDS CANNOT, MORE LIKE THE CAT I CONSUMED. MY CLAWS SCRATCH THE WALL, AND PLASTER CRUMBLES.

———  —  — · ·  —  —· —· —  ·  —  · ·  ———  ———  ———  —  — · —· ·

"What the fuck you think you doing, fag-boy?" Brett crossed his arms, tongue sliming over his hair-lip. I swear if he had a moustache, he'd twirl it. "Cruisin' for a bruisin'."

Yeah, I'm familiar with this song and dance. I'll never forget the time he flogged me on the jungle gym after school. The way my head thumped the pirate bridge, bouncing up to meet his fists again. Repeat. Bang. Repeat. Bang.

"I said, *what* are you doin'?"

My first instinct, of course, was to apologise. That's what people like me do—a survival technique. But something, maybe the buzz of handing Tina the mixtape in our old Christmas wrapping, made me stronger. Things came together, muscles within muscles re-knitting for the singular purpose of taking my nemesis head on. Bruises be damned.

"Not now, Brett," I said, making a move along the hall. He pinned me like a butterfly on a board in science class. Brett cocked his head, shaggy locks falling over his face. From this angle, a thatch of armpit hair could be seen behind the cusp of his shirt sleeve, a peekaboo of manliness that weirded me out. The feeling was jealousy.

"Don't touch me, Oldfield," I said, sounding more confident than I was.

"The fuck you say to me?"

I glared, fire in my eyes, wondering why guys like him were so mean to guys like me. Wasn't it exhausting to maintain anger for so long? Hair-lip aside (and even *that* was subjective), he was a good-looking dude, broad-shouldered and obviously (hair, ahem) on a puberty rollercoaster I'd be boarding soon. When he wasn't paying attention in class, if you caught him when his thoughts were occupied, you'd see Brett buckling under the pressure of tests, fear of failure announced in chewed pencils, torn strips of paper, tapping feet. More than once, I'd even felt sorry for him, an empathy that skirted close to self-defeat. Couldn't he see that I, on some level, gave a shit? Nope.

"I—I didn't say anything."

"Don't you fucking lie to me, *Heath*."

---

A SOUND ECHOES THROUGH THE HOUSE OF THE BOY WHO GIFTED ME MY ARCHITECTURE WITH HIS DESIRES.

THE OPENING AND CLOSING OF A DOOR. FOOTSTEPS.

THE HOLE IN THE WALL IS TWO FEET WIDE. A TIGHT FIT. CHUNKS OF BRICK PEPPER THE FLOOR ON EITHER SIDE, RUBBLE THAT I INHALE AND COUGH OUT. I STILL, LISTENING AS WHOEVER ENTERED THE BUILDING CLOMPS CLOSER TO THE DOOR AT THE TOP OF THE STAIRS.

I'M SALIVATING.

---

"Separate it, you two," said a passing teacher, Mrs Wolden, a rake of a woman dressed in earthy browns and greens. "Or are you both looking for a one-way ticket to detention?"

"No, Ms," I said, panting.

"And you, young Mister Oldfield?"

"Nope."

"Excuse me?"

"Fine," he said. "I'm buggering off!"

I took this as my cue to make a break for it. Mrs Wolden may have called at me to slow down, but those underwater sounds filled up the black and white school again, students zipping by. My backpack swung. Shoes skidded as I hung a sharp turn to cut across the yard, hoping Lincoln wouldn't see.

Tina Leoung sprawled on her back in a clearing, knapsack under her head, earphones on, a paperback above her face. The grass was dry as my throat. Warm wind blew between us, rustling dust-devils and old chip packets. I had to force all traces of Brett into submission as I mustered the bravery to open my mouth.

"Tina?"

She didn't hear. I took another step. My shadow slinked over her chest, and she tilted her head to see me. Lincoln's older sister didn't jump, as I would've if someone crept up on me like that. Tina: cool, calm, and collected. And pretty, of course.

*Wow*, I thought. *All the wows in the Milky Way.*

So many butterfly hair clips.

Tina ripped off her earphones, thumbed the Walkman, and rolled onto her stomach, smile the right-side up now. "What's happening, Heath?"

My affection was a zit that exploded on its own, words pulping from me in a rush. "Hey, Tina. I made you something and it would be awesome if you took it and I'll give it to you and you can listen to it or whatever. And. Yeah."

The crunch of Christmas wrapping under my grip.

"This is for me?"

A simple nod had never been more difficult.

"Heath, Heath, Heath." Gosh, the way she said it. A chiming bell. "Well, aren't you a total cute-pie."

Fearful I may vomit, I watched without believing as Tina raised her palm. Fingers bloomed. A flower just for me.

EXCITEMENT HAS ME UNCURLING FROM MY PLACE ON THE FLOOR, DISKS OF SPINE CLINKING INTO ALIGNMENT WITH THIS NEW SHAPE—ONE AS ALIEN AS THE THING AT THE TOP OF THE STAIRS. I SHUFFLE ABOUT AS I JIMMY OUT FROM BEHIND THE WASHING MACHINE, KNEEING THE TIN-DRUM.

"HELLO?" COMES THE VOICE.

SUNLIGHT ON MY FACE AS I SCUTTLE FORWARD. MY ARM PISTOLS TO BREAK A FALL, THE SYMMETRY OF BALANCE NOT YET MASTERED.

"WHO THE FUCK IS DOWN THERE?"

THESE WORDS HAVE A CADENCE THAT IS MORE INTIMIDATING THAN THE MAN-THING THEY ARE EJECTED FROM. HIS SONG IS A PATERNAL WARNING IN AN INDIFFERENT UNIVERSE, IMPULSES SEEKING ACKNOWLEDGEMENT THAT WILL NEVER BE HEARD ENOUGH, OR HUMOURED ENOUGH. IT WOULD HAVE BEEN BETTER FOR THE MAN-THING TO JUST DREAM AND WONDER, ACCEPTING HIS INSTINCTS FOR WHAT THEY WERE, BUBBLES IN THE GORE OF MY AFTERBIRTH. I TRACK HIS MOVEMENT AS HE TAKES ANOTHER STEP DOWN THE STAIRS. OH, HE'S FEARFUL. MY GULLET REFLECTS HIS CURIOSITY WITH THE IMITATION OF A SMILE. HE SEES ME THEN. I SAVOUR THE SWEETNESS OF HIS SHOCK.

"SWEET JESUS—"

I RESHAPE THE ATOMIC STRUCTURE OF THE AIR AS I DIVE, SO THE MAN-THING FEELS THE RUSH OF ME IN HIS DIAPHRAGM BEFORE I BITE. HE DROPS A BROWN PAPER BAG. IT BUSTS OPEN, AN APPLE TUMBLING PAST ME, GATHERING BRUISES. I CAN'T WAIT TO DIGEST THE MAN-THING, THE FATHER. MY IMPACT DROPS HIS JAW, SPILLING BLOOD I'LL LICK UP LATER. HE GURGLES SCREAMS INTO MY MOUTH AS I SUCK THE EYES FROM HIS FACE, OUR HARMONIES FLATTENING

INTO A HUM AS I ABSORB HIM, CALLOUSES TO CORE AND BEYOND.

THE TASTE OF HIM:

MEMORIES OF THE WOMAN HE JUST FUCKED, THE WOMAN WITH THE LONG RED HAIR, AND THE GUILT HE DOESN'T FEEL. SHE ASKS, "WHEN DO YOU THINK YOU'LL LEAVE YOUR WIFE?"

MEMORIES OF THE CHILDREN HE HAS, THE BOY AND THE GIRL. THE LOVE HE HAS FOR THEM. IN THEM, HE SEES BETTER VERSIONS OF HIMSELF THAT HE TRIES TO SHAPE WITH PRODS AND APPRAISALS. SOMETIMES, WHEN NOBODY IS AROUND, HE THINKS THE LOVE HE FEELS FOR THOSE TWO MIGHT KILL HIM.

MEMORIES OF HIS WIFE ON THEIR WEDDING DAY. CLOYING FLOWER SMELLS IN THE CHURCH. CANDLES. PEWS FILLED WITH PEOPLE TAKING PHOTOGRAPHS. HIS WIFE'S VEIL RISING TO REVEAL HER FACE. HE SMILES. HE SMILES TOO MUCH. AS HE SMILES EVERY DAY.

FINISHED, I WITHDRAW AND LICK MYSELF CLEAN, PEBBLED TONGUE OVER SKIN. BEFORE RETURNING TO THE DIG, I TASTE THE KNOWLEDGE I'VE SWALLOWED, AND TRY IT ON FOR SIZE.

"WHO THE FUCK IS DOWN THERE?" I MIMIC. "SWEET JESUS."

---

I didn't see Brett Oldfield again that day, which wasn't to say the hours went by easy.

Every passing second was one of his punches, a threat to fuck me up. At some point, the three-fifteen bell rang, and we leapt from our desks. If you could make it through Monday, you could make it through anything. Extra-curricular sports awaited some, afternoon cartoons for others. Almost all had chores to knock over, and we'd greet them gladly because anything was better than what we'd just slogged through.

I waited by the fence for my sister. Mum and Dad insisted we walk home together, no excuses. A bus pulled up by the curb, drawing students from cliques where comics and who-made-out-with-who gossip were traded.

A hand on my shoulder. I turned.

Hot wind blew from behind, billowing the uniform on Tina Leoung's slender frame. Earphones cupped her neck, cord trailing beneath her shirt and worming into the skirt pocket beneath. Her sunglasses made reading the expression on her face impossible, reflecting my shit-scared eyes instead.

"Hey, Tina." So calm and casual. Only not calm and casual at all.

As before, Tina lifted her palm, fingers uncurling to reveal the mixtape, this circle of suspense ending. So far as smiles go, mine was short-lived. *Take it back,* the gesture implied. *Minus the tacky gift-wrapping.* That added detail hurt and hurt worse because I knew how disappointed Mum would be in me. Taking the cassette in my hands without bursting into tears was one of the hardest things I'd ever done. But I did it. I got there.

"Heath," Tina said without a trace of animosity or condescension, just gentle sadness I didn't know how to resolve. "I listened to your tape, and I think you might be gay."

She walked away. I caught a whiff of her perfume.

I'm not sure what happened next. I know my sister tugged on my arm at some point to drag me off. My lizard brain got me home on a cloud of numb, passing all the familiar landmarks. The park nobody ever played at. The corner store I'd shoplifted from when I was ten. The railway tracks we laid coins on and waited for the trains to come along to flatten into something new.

It didn't occur to me until about an hour later that Dad's van had been parked in the driveway. But he wasn't home. He must have gotten back early and gone for a walk, or something. I went to the yard with a trowel from the garden, its blade rusted from having been left outside for so long, dropped to my knees and dug.

No worms. Just dry soil. Green ants scuttled across the Band-Aids on my knees. I brushed them aside, escaping bites. Finished, I set the trowel on the grass and rifled through my school shorts to withdraw the mixtape.

The cassette sat in my dusty palms, a dead thing with sprocket eyes. I flipped it over to take one last look at the plastic case with the sleeve marked with song titles I'd scribbled in a squishy font closer to the sides and bottom so everything would fit. I'd used a ballpoint pen and not one of my felt tips to ensure nothing would smear. That's how much I wanted Tina to know I cared. I'd even drawn a couple of butterflies under her name because they reminded me of her hair clips. I lowered it into the hole, and then filled the hole a scoop at a time. A dull heaviness filled the space where hope had been. But the hope of what? The hope that Tina, an older girl, my best friend's sister, would, what, fall in love with me, an eighth grader? That she'd want to go to Kellyville cinema or hold hands at lunchtime or kiss me under the stairs at the back of the school like other couples? It felt like it was my head now that was filled with ants. They chewed on me. Through me. I winced at the memory of her handing the cassette back to me, followed then by her words. Her sentence. That assumption. The way she thought she knew me, could tell who I was by what I liked.

In my life, I'd known embarrassment. A swimming carnival false start that sent me diving into the water, unaware that everyone was yelling at me to stop, that I was holding up the event until I reached the end of the fifty-metre pool, the other boys in the race laughing on their starting blocks.

I'd even known shame. Yes, I'd shoplifted from the corner store, but I'd also been caught. Mum found the $4.95 *Spawn* comic under my pillow, cornered me, wrestled out a confession before marching me down the street to hand the stolen goods back—and with the offer of sweeping the floors for a week. They accepted the offer, too. Ouch.

Tina and the mixtape was my first taste of humiliation.

"You stupid idiot," I whisper-yelled under my breath, smacking my temple. "Stupid-stupid-stupid! You stupid shit. You fuck. You c-word. You c-word. Shit. Shit. SHIT."

I stilled, gasping, became aware of the way I smelled: stinky with dried teen sweat. Repulsive. My eyes drifted across the yard, seeking distraction (from the chewing, chewing, chewing of the ants). There was the skeletal lemon tree in the corner, pathetic and quivering, all its leaves dead and dropped. A gate in the far corner that backed onto the alley where the garbage cans were collected. The fence dividing 6A Mason Drive from the vacant 6B wobbled in the breeze, too. A plastic bag rolled by: suburban tumbleweed.

"Heath?"

My chest seized at my sister's voice. She hung from the doorframe at the back of the house, monkey on a tree branch. A monkey in overalls—a weirdly comforting sight.

"Yeah?"

"I can't find Penny," she said.

We searched the house room by room, including the basement, but the family cat, like our father, was nowhere to be seen. "Maybe we let her out this morning when we were rushing," I said. "It'll be right. Penny'll come home when she's hungry."

"We're going to be in so much trouble."

"No, we won't, Dee. These things happen. They just do."

I marched upstairs to the bathroom. My uniform slopped on the tiles. Water ran in the shower. Before stepping into the stall, I went to the mirror above the sink and checked my armpits again. No progress. The mirror clouded over with steam. I thought about the mixtape under the earth in our backyard. Ants chewed again. They bit. I drew the plastic curtain back, stepped into the tub. Lowered my head to the stream and cried.

# EIGHT

"What do you mean your father's not home?"

Mum gripped her handbag in one fist, a plastic bag bulging with milk and bread in the other—things they had forgotten to buy the day before in Kellyville. Sweat beaded her face. She glared at me, the messenger to be shot down. Dee had been in front of the television on her chest watching *Beauty and the Beast* as though nothing were off kilter, though she may have been playing possum. I'll give her the benefit of the doubt because it didn't register with me that there might be something wrong until later, when everyone's doors were closed, and I did what I shouldn't have.

"We don't know where Penny is, either."

My mother expressed anger in the slamming of cupboard doors, the thumping of pots as she whipped up the dinner Dad had said he'd make. We ate in silence (not that I managed to get much down, Tina's accusation continued to wrestle within me), hours sluicing by, Dee and I shouting Penny's name as we rode up and down the street, clanking cans of cat food with forks to draw her in. We passed driveways where blue milk crates full of recyclable Saxby bottles waited to be picked up and returned to the factory by my father.

Dad's van remained in the driveway as darkness swept over

town and the streetlights blinked on, moths coming out to play. His keys were in the bowl by the front door among a knot of cords, cards, and receipts. Dad's work boots, however, were nowhere to be seen. We could only assume they were still on his feet.

Dee and I turned in.

After a while, I snuck downstairs. Thankfully, the door to Mum and Dad's room didn't open as I feared it might. I knew she was in there, and he wasn't.

Crickets droned through the windows. Even though we lived in the shifty part of town, we rarely battened down the hatches. You didn't have to enjoy where you lived to feel a curious—even abstract—trust in it, like those birds that hung out in the mouths of crocodiles. We'd had a kitty door installed out back—Penny's entry when she gave up hunting and slinked in with a sparrow for our slippers.

A breeze disturbed moonlit curtains, writhing shadows across the living room floor. I held my breath.

6A Mason Drive creaked. It always creaked in summer.

The stand where the rotary phone normally sat was empty, cord taut against the wall and trailing under the first door on the left. Turned out I wasn't the only thing creeping around in the dark. Mum's voice creeped, too. Spidery whispers itsy-bitsied from under the jamb and scurried into my ears.

My knees popped as I bent closer to the door.

"…I didn't come down in the last shower, Kat…" I heard her say.

Kat. Short for Aunty Katherine, Mum's sister.

"…I think he's gone back to *her*. That bitch. He's got so many secrets. You can see it in his face. I—I should've known it'd end up like this."

Back in bed, I rolled from shoulder to shoulder, watched by faces in the posters from movies I hadn't seen—the frightened woman, the bloodied hand. Whatever passion I'd had for them that morning was dimmer now, as though I'd poured too much of myself into that love too fast, the emptiness a foreign hollow in my core. I guessed growing up was the kind of thing you could measure in shirt sizes if you were so inclined, in hairs where there hadn't been hairs before, the kisses you wanted but never got. Only the maths didn't add up. Getting older was measured in the things you outgrew without realising it, in all the stuff you thought would never not be important, yet you leave behind piece by piece.

The upper corner of one poster peeled away from the wall.

I didn't care enough to correct it.

---

I AM THE FACE IN THE BACK OF YOUR DOOR THAT WATCHES YOU WHEN YOU SLEEP. YOU DON'T HEAR ME BECAUSE YOUR DREAMS HAVE YOU, NOT YOU, THEM. I LONG TO SIT AND WATCH YOU BREATHE. IT ISN'T TIME THOUGH. I'M TOO EARLY, TOO UNFORMED. BUT I AM A PATIENT THING. THE ATOMS OF YOUR DOOR, THE MOLECULES OF THIS ROOM, WE DANCE AND MELD. THAT'S EASIER FOR NOW.

YOU GAVE ME THIS POWER.

THERE ARE DOORS EVERYWHERE, CHILDLING.

THINK ABOUT IT. WHEN ARE YOU EVER WITHOUT ONE? I'VE INVESTIGATED WHAT COMES AHEAD, AND SEEN YOU LYING WITH LOVERS IN DIRTY UNDERPASSES. I'VE SEEN YOU AT YOUR WORST AND MOST WEAK. YOUR FEAR OF OTHERS, YOUR VANITY, YOUR NEED TO UPHOLD YOUR PRIDE—WILL ENSURE I'M ALWAYS WITH YOU. YOU'RE A HIDER. NOT THAT IT MATTERS TO ME (TO US). WE ARE THE DOOR, THE WOOD IT'S MADE FROM, THE WATER THAT FED IT, THE AIR YANKING IT FROM THE SOIL, THE SUN THAT GAVE IT ENERGY, THE ENERGY THAT KEEPS WORLDS SPINNING. YOU DON'T NEED TO ASK TO BE SACRIFICED TO BE THE SACRIFICE. WE ARE THE 2 AND THE 4 AND THE 8. I'VE INVESTIGATED WHAT COMES. YOUR SCARS SPELL IT OUT CLEAR.

DO YOU KNOW YOU TALK IN YOUR SLEEP NOW AND YEARS FROM NOW, WHEN YOU'RE SLEEPING OUTSIDE WITH A PACK UNDER YOUR HEAD, WHEN YOU'RE SLEEPING IN A HOTEL ROOM YOU PAID FOR WITH $250 A WOMAN NAMED MARGE GAVE YOU? YOU MENTION A NAME. "MUM," YOU SAY.

I'D WELCOME HER, YOU KNOW. I'D CRYSTALLISE YOUR 'MUM' AND KEEP HER IN THE BLACK BETWEEN DEAD STARS. HER NAME HAS A TEXTURE. I WONDER IF IT HAS A TASTE, TOO?

MUM.

YOU WILL TRY TO OUTRUN ME, BURN ME, REPLACE ME WITH THINGS THAT REFLECT INSTEAD OF ABSORB. I WILL FIND YOU. YOU WILL ROT IN WAYS I NEVER WILL, AND ONE DAY YOUR LEGS WON'T WORK LIKE THEY USED TO. YOUR BOWELS WILL DO YOU IN. THE PEOPLE YOU THOUGHT YOU COULD TRUST WON'T BE AROUND WHEN YOU NEED THEM MOST, WHEN I COME BACK TO YOUR BED AND AM STRONG ENOUGH TO BREATHE IN YOUR EXHALES. THAT'S WHERE I'LL FIND YOU. I AM EVERYWHERE, EVEN THOUGH MY POWER DIMS, ONLY TO HAVE IT COME BACK STRONG. HUNGER DRAINS. FEEDING REPLENISHES. WE'RE NOT THAT DIFFERENT. JUST HOW IT GOES, HEATH. TONIGHT, IN YOUR ROOM, FROM YOUR DOOR, I'M WEAK. IT WON'T STAY THAT WAY FOR LONG, THOUGH.

I AM THE FACE IN THE BACK OF THE DOOR THAT WATCHES YOU WHEN YOU SLEEP. YOU KEEP ME YOUNG IN WAYS I DON'T UNDERSTAND, OR NEED TO UNDERSTAND. YOU KEEP ME RAVENOUS.

HERE'S A CHALLENGE: I DEFY YOU NOT TO LET THE DREAMS COME AND SAY HER NAME AGAIN.

MUM. MUUMMMMMMM.

I AM THE FACE IN THE BACK OF YOUR DOOR THAT WATCHES YOU WHEN YOU SLEEP.

---

Cartoon stars glowed green against black, reminding me of where and who I was. The dream I'd woken from withdrew fast. Memories lingered among the glow-in-the-dark star stickers on my bedroom ceiling. Dad helped put them up three years earlier. They came on a slip of waxy paper inside an astrology magazine from school, but the subscription lapsed and only two months' worth made it to us students in the end. An incomplete galaxy I'd long ago stopped caring about.

My dry throat clenched. Neck bones cracked as I turned to look out the window. Night lurked behind the flyscreen, wire mesh moving in and out. The dark breathed.

*Yes. I'm me again. I'm me. And I'm wet.*

I sat up, trying to force my lungs into rhythm, tickling all over. Fingers slipped beneath the elastic pull of my boxer shorts to confirm what I already knew.

"Damn it." I studied plastic stars once more, wiped my fingers on the *Star Wars* sheets, smearing what the guys at school called 'cum', or 'sprog' (yuck), or worse, 'population paste' (a descriptor that not only weirded me out but frightened me—no wonder I felt guilty, all those wasted lives).

Unease writhed through me.

Waking had shattered the dream. I tried to piece it together best I could, but not all the fragments were there.

*A naked man by the window. Daylight bright behind him. His sculptured chest. The flat V of muscle funnelling down to his stomach, to his cock.*

Blackness.

*The naked man, Clayton, approaches the bed. His shadow climbs my feet—only they aren't my feet. They are too big and have callouses on the heels.*

Blackness.

*His silhouette flows closer, an arm reaching out, touching the leg that isn't mine—yet I experience his touch as if this is my skin. He says something, climbs onto the mattress, into the glow of the bedside lamp.*

Blackness.

*He touches me. I see him. Only it's not Clayton McManus any more.*

*It's a tall woman. She's naked. I see the heart shaped birthmark above her left breast. The woman has long red hair that reaches down to her waist. She says something.*

"When do you think you'll leave your wife?"

I slinked into the bathroom to scrub my shorts clean. Turned on the light. Brightness hurt my eyes. I did it anyway—maybe I deserved the hurt. Suds churned between fingers. Cleaning my body did no good. The rabbit hole deepened, a warren of sticker stars and the smashed-mirror-face of the dream man who made me feel something that wasn't healthy. Something that was obviously wrong. That wrongness killed people in foggy bowling lanes where the Grim Reaper sometimes played, on the news before my parents changed the channel, clearing their throats and shifting in their recliner chairs.

*This can't be happening. Please God. Not me. I'm so scared.*

Finished, I closed the door, sick to my stomach. Even though I'd wrung them out best I could, the shorts were still damp. I tip-toed to the window to drape them over the sill, hopeful I'd wake early enough to retrieve them before anyone came in (little sisters and mothers never knocked, as though barging in were part of the deal).

I glanced down at the lawn. Wind blew, rattling the gate in the fence. A dog barked. The moonlit patch of dirt where I'd buried my secret.

Even though my parents sent us to Catholic school, and trundled us off to church on Sundays, I wasn't sure I believed in God. I dropped to my knees and prayed just in case.

*Don't let this be me. I don't* want *this to be me. Love is in the Air. Love is in the Air! See, I'm okay with the song now. I want a girlfriend. I'm going to get married, just like Mum and Dad and everyone else on TV and in town and like my teachers. I need to be normal. Please, please God. I'll do anything you want. I'll be a priest when I grow up, I'll donate to the poor, whatever. Just don't let this be true. It wasn't my dream. Bad magic put it there. I'm not a fag. Why would Tina even say that? I wanted to ask her out. What is it about me that's so easy for others to read? I need to mask up. I need to hide better. But I've got nothing to hide! Ouch. Everything hurts. Say it isn't true, this thing I hadn't even thought of before. Never. Not even once. I'm shocked. God, I want to* be *the man in the dream. I don't* want *the man in the dream. Him. Clayton. You've got it back the front. You've got it all wrong.*

I felt watched and was comforted.

---

I AM THE FACE IN THE BACK OF THE DOOR THAT WATCHES YOU AS YOU PRAY.  AND I AM A PATIENT THING.

# SEVEN

That sick-to-my-stomach feeling from the night before crawled inside me again during class where I'd been staring at the ceiling fans instead of the chalkboard. It was with me the whole day, as I dodged Brett Oldfield at recess and lunch and pretended to be present when people spoke at me. Every part of me thumped. Hot-hot-hot. I imagined a dentist using pliers to force an infected tooth into my bellybutton, skin yielding to swallow the abscess root and all.

*Someone make this better.*

I wished I could punch out the hurt like Brett Oldfield had done that day on the jungle gym, his knuckles against the back of my head so the bruises were harder to see (not that I'd tell Mum and Dad—better cracking headaches than being seen for what I was: someone who didn't know how to defend himself). *I hurt,* spoke the force in Brett's punches, *so you'll hurt, too.* The cosmic balance bullies think they bring, and my part to play in that balance.

I told Lincoln about Dad and Penny between classes, my voice shaking.

"Jesus, Spoons. That sounds hectic as," he said. "How about I come over later on my bike and help put up missing posters, or something?"

"Posters for my Dad?"

"No, dude," he said, incredulous. "For your cat."

After school, Dee and I completed the figure 8 of the day by walking home in silence. Distracted though we were, we avoided stepping on cracks in the concrete for fear we would fall and break our grandmother's backs. Not that we had grandmothers. Nanna Spooner had passed away the year before. I'll never forget the funeral, how Dad wept—huge, almost cartoonish sobs. Mum squeezed our knees so we knew things would be okay. I'd expected the casket to be open. Something in the back of my head told me it was closed for the benefit of us kids. I resented that. Being underestimated.

"Do you think he'll be home by now?" Dee asked.

I snapped at my sister in an unfair older brother voice. "Stop asking so many *bloody* questions!"

"Don't you shout at me, Heath. I didn't do this to us. I only asked one question."

We walked in silence for a while. Silence I broke.

"I'm sorry," I said. "I'm not feeling well is all."

Dee sighed. Shuffled her feet. "Well, maybe Dad took Penny to the vet," she said, only without a trace of conviction. "Maybe she wasn't feeling well, too."

*(I think he's gone back to her. The bitch. I should've known it'd end up like this…)*

"I don't know, Dee."

*(Secrets).*

We came down our street and stopped in our tracks. A police van was parked behind Dad's vehicle in the driveway. Another car sat at the curb, too. The paintjob, the dented grill, beamed recognition into my brain.

"Aunt Kat," I said, turning to Dee. She locked eyes with me.

Under any other circumstances, the sight of Mum's sister's car would have sent us into a sprint. Because we knew at the other end of our dash there would be warm Aunt Kat hugs and the chocolate bars she brought with her when she visited. On that day, however, the presence of all three vehicles evoked a chill. The poisoned tooth in my stomach froze and cracked, seeping anxiety through me. It was getting harder to breathe.

You'd struggle to find two women more different. Kat made up for Mum's aloofness threefold, and when she gifted you with one of her hugs, you became the most important person in the universe, someone who didn't need to be challenged or told to clean their room or grow up (and why would you ever want things to change when the alternative was to remain in her arms forever, curtains of silver hair falling over you, the fluffy smell of the fabric softener she washed her clothes in filling your senses).

But whatever happened while we were at school had erased the smile that defined her. A large, broken woman with wet eyes behind vintage spectacles stood in her place instead. She'd aged since the last time we'd seen her. Maybe she was shrinking, too. Or maybe I'd just gotten taller.

"Missed you too, Heath," she said. "Both of you."

"Where's Mum?" Dee asked.

"Oh, you sweet dove, you. Your mother's in the kitchen with Louis Demeeter. Let's allow them to sit a little while longer."

"Louis the policeman?" I said. "This is about Dad, isn't it?"

Kat invited us into our mother's room, groaning as she sat on the bed, resting a cane across her lap. "Yes, it is. Mum's upset right now. That's why I've come for a spell."

Dee toyed with her skirt. "Where are you going to sleep? Do you want to bunk with me? It'll be squishy but that's okay."

"The couch will do me fine. I'll be staying for as long as all this business takes. See, sweet dove, we—we—don't know where your father is. He didn't come back today either. And his boss called, said he didn't report in for work."

"W-what does that mean?" I said.

Aunt Kat's fingers, ornamented in rings that looked like they had been raided from toy vending machines at Kellyville mall, grabbed her cane. Squeezed. Skin over wood, knuckles turning white.

"I'm going to talk to you both like adults, okay?" she said. "You've got to be strong for one another, and for my sister." Her next breath made the room smaller. Walls inched in, Mum and Dad's tallboy towering over us. "We can't officially file a missing person's report for another twenty-four hours, but if Dad's not back by then, well, that's what we'll be doing. You know Louis. We all do. Your mum and I even went to school with him and his brothers, before I moved away to James Bridge. Good people, he is, our Louis. You can't say that about everyone. He's here as a favour, came out of the goodness of his heart when your mum called to walk us through things a'step at a'time. Because who knows what to do when this kind of thing happens? *Who*, I ask?"

"Did you tell Louis about Penny?" Dee asked.

"Penny?"

"Our cat, Aunt, uh, Kat," I said, snorting half a giggle. "She's missing as well."

"That beautiful tabby of yours? You got photo of her I can pinch?"

"There are photos Dad took hanging on the memory wall by the stairs, and some blurry ones in the drawer by the front door," I told her. "Is this for posters? My friend Lincoln Leoung wants to help us."

"Well, thank God in heaven for the kindness of the Lincoln Leoungs of this world. We're going to zip over to the newsagency and get **LOST** copies made lickedy-split before they close for the day. I didn't bring chocolate with me this time, left too quick for that. So, we'll get ice-cream on the way home. How's that sound to—"

"I'm heading off now," said Louis Demeeter from the doorway, muscled arms resting on either side of the architrave. The gun hanging from his slender waist caught my eye and I found myself wondering if Louis—'our Lewis,' as Aunt Kat called him—had ever killed anyone. "Afternoon, kids. Your aunt here brought you up to speed then?"

We nodded.

"It's important you tell Mum or Aunt Kat straight away if you see your father," he said. "If he shows up at school be sure to talk to your teacher and have Principal Dahl ring your mother at work straight away. Understand?"

We nodded again.

"No need for us to go all red-alert yet. That goes for you as well, Kat. But this is well and truly on my radar. I'll be checking in. Soon enough, you'll be sick of the sight of me."

"Say no such thing, Louis—oh, I mean 'Officer Demeeter'." Aunt Kat elbowed me. "*La-dee-da.*"

"You hear the way she talks to me?" Louis smiled. "No respect for authority. Good thing we've got you two kids to do the heavy liftin' round here. Correct?"

I offered a salute. He made me feel safe.

"That's the spirit, Heath. Did I hear you say you're heading out, Kat?"

Kat moaned as she stood and limped over to give her old friend a hug. "Maybe we should all soldier on together."

"Can I say hello to Mum first?" Dee asked. "I think she'd like that."

"After ice-cream," Louis said. "Everything's better after ice-cream."

---

Lincoln buzzed about on his bicycle, weaving between the trees, the telegraph and power poles we'd stapled our **LOST CAT** photocopies to. Real trees, I had to remind myself. Real telegraph and real power poles. These were real photocopies that we'd hung.

Only nothing felt real.

When the time came to lodge a missing person's report as Louis—no, Officer Demeeter—had explained, would we march this same stretch of road to post pictures of Dad? Which image from the memory wall would we use? One with him on his own? One where Mum had been cropped out, so she didn't have to share the frame with the man who'd hurt her? Because yes, there *had* been hurt in every inch of her that morning as we readied ourselves for the day. I could see that now.

Dad hurt Mum by being with her, 'the bitch'.

Another secret for me to keep.

The urge to throw the stapler in my hands intensified. I held this frustration in check and glared at the sky through the trees. It was the time of the year when the days held their light too desperately, stretching twilight to its limit. The first stars like tiny punctures. Soon, blood-hungry mosquitoes would come.

"Lincoln," Kat called from the path ahead where she'd stopped to rest on her cane. "Time for you to head back to your place before it gets dark." Our aunt's mobility wasn't the greatest on account of her long-term battle with diabetes. She called this illness her 'big old type twos.' I had no idea what that meant.

Bike tyres screeched to a halt at my side.

"You going to be okay, Spoons?" my friend said.

"Yeah, I'll be cool."

Dee walked along the curb, a circus performer daring the tightrope. Not listening but listening always.

Aunt Kat turned to Lincoln again, smiling. "You'll see Heath tomorrow. Bless you for coming with us. Little things like that have a way of comin' back 'round. Paying it forward is what it's called."

Lincoln smiled and refocused on me. "You'll be in class tomorrow, Spoons?"

"Will I, Aunt?" I asked.

"You and Dee both will be. It'll give your mother and me some quality sister time. It's nice for us oldies to be alone, especially when times are tough."

Lincoln stared, wanting to talk about something without others around. I hoped that 'something' concerned the situation we'd found ourselves in and not certain things his sister may have revealed. Looking back, I'm sure it was the former. Over the space of a few days, our timelines had become disjointed, a fracture in the bone of our friendship that **LOST** posters and a decent catch-up weren't going to rectify. I was older than I'd been at the beginning of that week. And I'm sure Lincoln saw that. Being left behind always hurt.

He jumped on his bike. Gone with a wave, mosquitoes in pursuit.

Dee, Aunt Kat, and I walked home. Bats flew overhead. Birds returned to their nests, paving the sidewalk with scat. We passed a house on the left that I would have otherwise avoided. Brett Oldfield lived there with his parents and older brothers.

We kept our heads down and marched on. Aunt Kat didn't just lead the way. Her silence and the tap-tap-tap of her cane implied we hold course and wisely choose our battles. We chose to ignore the yells and sounds of breaking plates coming from within the old weatherboard house we left behind.

---

Later that night, Mum visited me in my room. I'd heard voices from down the hall as she exchanged words with Dee before joining me.

"Are you okay?"

"We'll talk tomorrow," she said, her kiss cold.

I let her go, not calling her back even though I longed to. The night wound on without sounds sieving from downstairs. The temptation to skulk around for another eavesdropping session poked and prodded. Mum would talk when she was ready, something I'd have to respect. She deserved that.

---

Noises like clammy fingers over a rubber birthday balloon woke me.

*Switch on the bedside lamp*, said my brain. *But you can't, can you? You're frozen.*

What if it wasn't just a trick of shadows? Without a sense of what was actual and what was imagined, how could anyone expect me to be strong? Screaming was too easy a way out of whatever I felt. Everything clamped shut, locking it all in. I trembled.

*Please, no.*

*(You can do this.)*

*I don't want to.*

*(Man up, Heath. Man up.)*

Teeth clenched, I pushed against the knot of fear that trapped me and stretched my hand across the no-man's land between the edge of the mattress and the bedside table, a gap monsters I'd convinced myself didn't hide in *might* lurk. Maybe I was wrong on that count, too. Maybe parents everywhere had been misled. Oz might be real. Santa might shuffle down your chimney after all. And the monsters under your bed might be waiting for you to grow comfortable in your disbelief before proving you more wrong than you've ever been, a correction of tooth and claw. And the Grim Reaper's bowling ball.

I hit the lamp. Moths shot out of the night to freckle the flyscreen, dusty grenades with twitching legs.

A skeletal branch had grown out of the wall opposite me, forcing a movie poster onto the floor in the process. And not a sapling, either.

A whole, partial tree.

I threw the sheets back and tip-toed across the room, still vibrating, the same shivering hand that braved the lamp now braving the tree. Disbelief, I learned, was the taste when you put your tongue on the end of a battery. Bitter. A bit like poison. The tree hadn't grown *through* the wall, as weeds grow through cracks in cement. No. This thing was born *of* the wall. Its bark twisted with splinters and thorns, pained in a way, strangled by its own self. It bore fruit, too. Fat lemons.

*(Breathe, Heath.)* Only that wasn't the worst thing. *(Breathe!)*

The tree in the wall of my bedroom was decorated with thin black audio cassette tape.

*No*, I thought. *Please, no.*

I leapt forward to snatch at the knots of tape. The branches pulled this way and that, dangling the secret that had been purged back to me while I slept. A lemon plopped to the floor, exploding pulp and churning maggots. I flung the coils of tape under my bed, panting, expecting eyes to blink at me from the shadows, and scuttled around to face the closed door.

"MUM!"

An answer resonated through 6A Mason Drive, followed by thudding feet. Dee called. The door banged open, and my mother ran into the room with Aunt Kat at her side. She stopped. Quiet between us. Her eyes were wide.

"Come here," Mum said. "Now, Heath."

And I obeyed.

"Get back, Dee," Aunt Kat said to that silhouette in the hall.

"What's going on? Is Heath okay?" Dee asked. "Is it Dad? Is he back?"

Mum turned to her sister. "Go sit with her for a while, Kat. And close the door."

I watched something unspoken pass between the two older siblings, invisible lightning zapping my aunt into action. She left us, her cane tap-tap-tapping as she went.

Alone now, I spoke to my mother in whispers. "What is that thing?"

Part of me wanted to know the answer. Another part just wanted to hear my voice, to try it on for size in a new world where things like this were possible. Another lemon hit the floorboards, bursting. We both watched the maggots wriggle, all manic smiles and frowns. Tiny puckering sounds.

"You're sleeping in my room tonight," she said, her voice low and even. Mum led me from the room, stopping to glance at the tree one last time before easing the door shut.

In the hot darkened hallway, my mother stopped. She exhaled and crouched in front of me. Her eyes were wet and shimmery. "You saw it, right?" she said. "In the wall."

"Yeah," I said. "This is happening, Mum."

She took me by the chin and held my gaze. I saw her looking at me like she sometimes looked at Dad, searching for secrets below the surface. Ready to not believe whatever came next.

---

Dee joined Mum in her bed, tight as sardines under a sheet. I was curled up on the floor with a blanket over my legs, a hard pillow under my head. My sister snored. *No nightmares for her.* The upright fan studied us in the corner, spinning blades glimmering. I could hear my mother thinking from the other side of the bed. I wondered if she remained awake due to fright, or if she was keeping watch. Her breathing never slowed.

*Exploded fruit. Maggot kisses.*

I made to leave the room.

Mum sat up fast enough to startle me. The combination of hot air and blue moonlight turned her hair into seaweed writhing on her scalp.

"Where are you going?" As to how her voice could be hushed and yet so firm, I'd never know. "Back to bed. You'll wake Dee. You can bunk up with us if you want."

My hand reached for the handle.

"Heath?" she said. "Are you listening?"

Emptiness gnawed at my middle.

"I'm starving, Mum. I'm so hungry it hurts."

# SIX

"Tell them it's a tree," Mum yelled at sister who was speaking into the phone in the hall. "A fucking tree. Not a branch. Not a twig. Not a root or anything. A tree."

"Suppose you heard that?" Kat said into the receiver. I watched the way she propped her walking stick under one elbow, resting her weight against the wall with the other, her dress glowing in the new light. She was on the line with our landlord, Vicky—or maybe it was Vicky's husband whose name I could never remember even though I'd met him a dozen times. He with the moustache and red wine teeth.

A wormy moustache. A maggoty moustache.

My stomach clenched. I ate every bit of my breakfast and still wanted more.

Mum refused to let me go back into my room. It was she who went in to get my school bags and clothes while Aunt Kat prepared food downstairs. Our aunt had made bacon, eggs, and fried tomatoes for us.

"Okay, Vicky," Kat said with a sigh. "I understand. I'll let my sister know. Yeah, that'll have to do. We'll see you tomorrow then. Thank you. 'Bye."

She slotted the receiver into its holster, the bell issuing a faint ding.

"Are they coming to take it away?" I asked, slinging on my backpack.

"They'll be here tomorrow," Kat told Mum. "They're up the coast and would rather come themselves rather than just sending in the clowns. I'm not sure she got what I was saying, though. Can't blame her. We must've sounded mad as hatters."

"Maybe we *are* mad," Mum said. "Dee, would you stop dragging the chain. You'll be late for school."

My sister marched into the room, furious. "This is *stupid*—I *hate* all this stuff—*what's* going on—and *where* is my Dad?"

Mum fingered her brow. "Kat," she said, exasperated.

"Come here, sweet dove." Our aunt offered her hand to my sister, who took it. "Your mother's under a lot of stress right now, so let's all cut her a break. I'll get you kids to school in the aunty-mobile."

We trudged to the front door, lunch bags crunched in our fists. Feet pattered behind us and we three turned to find Mum in the doorway between the living room and kitchen, her hands on either side of the architrave, echoing Louis Demeeter, sucking in hot air. Her eyes were scratches. "Hurry back, Kat." She sounded scared.

Ouch. All the ouches in the Milky Way.

I handed my lunch to Dee and crossed to where my mother stood. I offered to stay home and help her in any way I could. She quieted me with a kiss. I couldn't stand seeing her so frightened. My insides screeched in a noiseless, elemental way.

"Thanks, darl'," she said. "But it's best you and your sister steer clear of here until the police are through with me. I've got to screw my head on right again."

"I want to help, Mum. I mean it."

Kat escorted Dee from the room, leaving us be.

"I know you do. You *are* a help."

Maintaining eye contact proved harder than I'd thought it would be. I forced myself to do it. There had never been anything more important than this. "One thing and then I'll go."

"Come on, Heath. You'll be late."

"Do you think Dad is with another lady?" I said. "Is that where you think he is?" And then I asked her, went all the way, even though I hadn't planned or wanted to, the question smoking up from somewhere inside me, a furnace in my deepest part that had been building heat for a while. "With the lady who has long red hair?"

Outside, Kat beeped the aunty-mobile, making Mum and I flinch. I held my ground. Mum needed to know I was older than she saw me as, and that if our father, her husband, was going to be with the woman with the red hair, the bitch, then I had to step up.

"You don't have to tell me," I said. A flutter of guilt dimmed the fire. "Sorry if I've made you sad. Talk to me about it later if you want."

Mum's face was a shield. I made for the front door, passing the wall where photographs were arranged. My reflection passed over those rectangles of glass, windows into the family we used to be.

"Heath?"

Outside heat reached for me. I stopped, turned.

"Never mind," she said, tears in her eyes.

---

While my body may have been tucked behind a string of graffiti-tattooed desks at school, undersides pebbled with gum my kneecaps sometimes touched, my mind wandered to Top Video Universe. The fantasy was slippery, though. And in it, the shop was closed.

This image ripped me back to the classroom where Mrs Wolden moved her mouth but no sound came out. Ceiling fans beat hot exhales over us. A girl scribbled a *I heart So-and-So* into her pencil case. Someone scrubbed a page with an eraser, blowing shavings onto the floor. I'd grown up with these kids, only brain fog hazed their names.

Lunch bell rang. I let the crowd push me this way and that. Slammed a locker. Spat into the courtyard. Both shoulders clipped at the same time by girls running from one quadrangle to another. Searched faces for a glimmer of Dad, skimming the ground to see if Penny wove through all those knee-high socks. I avoided Lincoln, who sat under a tree with students chowing sandwiches. Hi-C and Boku juice boxes everywhere, straws twisted into knots. Toxic Crusader cards traded. Yoyos whizzed. Concern etched my best friend's expression as he looked for me.

Wind ushered me into yet another stream. I followed rolled-up trash around the back of the main building. Heat radiated off the redbrick façade. Outlines of children drawn in chalk on the bitumen like a crime scene awaiting bodies.

Brett Oldfield sat there, head in hands, hair greasy and kneecaps pinched in an upturned V. On any other day, I would have run for the hills.

I shuffled onto the ground near him, gravel crunching, unsure of what I was doing but knowing it felt right. It had to be him who broke the silence, either by threat or invitation. Strange as it was, I wanted to stay, preferred his presence to Lincoln's. Brett appeared to be the only person at St Bridget's as crushed as me.

"My folks told me there was cops at your place yesterday," he said without glancing up. "They saw them on their way home from work."

"Uh-huh."

"That's fucked up, dude."

"Uh-huh."

Crows circled, shadows on concrete. Beyond that concrete, which ended in a straight line, grass busied all the way to the road to Kellyville. Mountains beyond. And thunderheads beyond them.

"My dad's missing," I confessed.

Brett shifted his weight against the wall. I noticed how his muscles moved beneath his shirt, tensing and releasing, hints at hurt he could inflict on me. Was I supposed to feel gratitude at his restraint? That didn't strike me as healthy at all. If only gratitude was the sole thing I'd felt that day.

His brown eyes peered from within a ring of purple and yellow bruise. And then I remembered the shouts coming from his house. The sounds of breaking plates.

Something fluttered in my guts, an itch that reminded me of those times when I daydreamed about slipping behind the beaded curtain at Top Video Universe. That itchiness was a trap. The feeling was dirty, an adult wrongness. My fists clenched. Brett's muscles under his shirt, his brown eyes. Yeah, shame was much easier.

"You're lucky," he said before getting up to leave.

*Smashing plates. Yelling.*

Lucky? Was that what he said? A hundred strings in me snapped at once—no, not strings. Cassette tape innards. My self-control peeled back, and everything flared in my head. I wasn't reclining against the wall any more, but on my feet.

Brett spun to face me.

My hands latched around his throat. I didn't know what I was doing or why. A part of my brain thought I might have reached out to kiss him. Only this was worse—maybe.

He forced me back, but my grip was stronger. A shock to us both. More tape tore away behind my eyes. The urge to squeeze squeezed back, fuelled by power I didn't understand or question. It was a hunger, something that had been building since returning from Kellyville. Brett lifted a knee and crunched me in the balls. Pain registered somewhere.

*I hissed.*

I hissed at him like a cat. My breath stunk of dead under-the-house things.

"STOP," I screamed at myself.

My fingers let go and Brett hit the ground. He scampered onto his haunches and bounced away, coughing and spurting. I expected him to come for me. The only thing Brett punched was the air. He ran away, giving me the finger.

My hands dropped, lifeless things without purpose. These hands used to draw. I turned to study the faraway road, the mountains, and clouds. No artist could capture such enormity, let alone me—so why even try? Why try *anything*? This wasn't just about Dad and Penny, or about how accurate Tina's words were. This was about the otherness that had crept into my life and body. Although I couldn't name it or tell you what it looked like (yet), I felt its enormity and age, and was afraid.

"What's happening?" I said. Clouds answered.

Lightning split the bright day, only no thunder followed. Just an eerie quiet and the ripple of electric air. Hairs along my neck stood on end. I doubled over and vomited. The muscles of my stomach clambered for the last of whatever poison was in the pit, forcing up bile. There was none of the relief that being sick brings, only an emptiness that could never be truly emptied so long as whatever was happening continued.

I coughed up a silver ring.

It peered at me from the bitumen. I didn't have to read the inscription on the inside of the silver band to recognise that it belonged to my father.

"N-no," I said, snatching it up.

Clouds churned and swelled hail green. I wished for the release of thunder. Thunder was normal and scientific and bound in rules. Panicked, I picked up the slippery ring and threw it into the field, watched it vanish in the long grass swishing and swaying in the wind, combed as if by an unseen hand.

I wiped my face and ran around the side of the building as the end of lunch bell chimed across the quadrangle where there were patches of grass students weren't allowed to walk across because it had, for some reason, been blessed by priests. Cliques stood, brushing yard grit off their uniforms. Brett huddled in the shade of the church where we used to be marked for the *quality* of our confessions by a priest who now spends his days in prison. The bully noticed me, and in full view of everyone, screamed in my direction.

"You fuggin' faggot freak!" His raspy voice wisped from the cleft of his hair-lip.

All faces in that quadrangle looked at Brett. Beat. And then in unison, everyone turned to me. There was no question who his cry had been directed at. The bell rang a final time. Dry wind rustled old wrappers. The cry of a crow.

"Brett Oldfield, come here this very minute," shouted Mrs Wolden.

I watched the long-legged teacher lope towards him, moving like pasta in a pot of boiling water, my cue to run. The boy's bathroom was the perfect place to fantasise I didn't exist. I stood in front of mirrors, the stink of urinal cakes thick in my nostrils, and doused myself in water, running my shaggy locks of brown hair under the tap. Tried to reel my breathing in. The drain was a black eye with something slinking inside it, something down deep. My fingers gripped the porcelain, heartbeat climbing again. A couple of boys busied behind me, stopping to stare. I overheard whispers with my name shoehorned in.

"Got something to say to me?" I said, turning on them, my voice breaking on 'say', and that break echoing. None of the guys answered, raising hands to ward me off. Their laughs felt like shards of glass in my flesh.

I locked myself within a stall where grout between the tiles was filled with the names of students and movie quotes in ballpoint ink, and sat on the toilet, telling myself this wasn't—couldn't be— happening. Only it *was* happening. Just like I told Mum. The urge to vomit rushed back but passed after I pinched the skin under the hem of my shorts.

Soft flab between my fingers.

Twisted, pain a kind of release.

Calmer, I emerged from of the stall and noticed the washbasin. Green ants marched from the drain in a spiral. Surely, they lived behind the bathroom walls, maybe forced from a nest by a leaking pipe. My brain wouldn't let that option hold. My brain told me these ants came from the hole I'd dug in our yard, and like the tree that emerged in my room to return what I'd tried to bury, they followed me here for a reason: to ensure I knew that hiding wasn't an option. Truth would find me wherever I went.

Fingers curled around my wrist when I shuffled outside. I spun, expecting to find Brett, fist raised and ready to knock my teeth out. To my surprise, it was Tina, a group of snickering girls by the lockers behind her.

"Heath," Tina said, eyes brimming with concern. Her grip tightened.

"Not now. Please—"

"I just wanted to say I'll defend you," she said, conspiratorial and hushed.

"What? Defend me? What does that even mean, defend me?" Sympathy radiated off her, not that I'd asked for it. Worse, it felt closer to pity. "Why do I need defending, Tina?"

"I'll defend you when they say things," she told me.

It was as though I could feel every blood cell in my body expanding.

"How dare you," I said, vision drawing to a point, a closing iris in an old movie. "I didn't *ask* you to do that. I don't *want* you to do that. Jesus, Tina, all I did was give you a mixtape. That's all. You should've kept your thoughts about me to yourself. I didn't ask for any of this. I don't want it. Fuck it. I'm not fucking—"

*Not fucking gay.*

I couldn't even say it.

"Oh, Heath," Tina said, drawing back her hands and crossing them in front of her chest. "I'm so sorry." Or at least that's what I thought she said. I'd walked away by then, the pounding in my ears back, thrashing the headache to life again.

My skin stayed dewy in our final class of the day, frog-like with water and sweat under my shirt. Fingernails dug into the wooden desk. Teeth ground. *Pound-pound-pound-pound-pound.* I glanced at the students around me, so desperate for validation with their hands raised, others bored into a stoop. Boys with grass-stained shirts passed notes. Girls accepted them. Feet tapped. The occasional glimpse in my direction.

A spike of clarity.

There was none of me in them.

We'd grown up together, been in each other's homes for parties, heard each other fart and seen each other cry and bleed. Now, they were aliens. I saw girls who would grow up and get married, some having children of their own. Boys who would devolve into men who forgot it was okay to break down. I saw sports I didn't know the rules to and careers that were a lot like cannibalism. They were cold things. All of them, frozen.

The thought steamed, revealing Mrs Wolden in the doorway on the other side of the room. She announced my name for everyone to hear. She said it twice. Students strained in their chairs, watching me swallow and deliberate and yield. I stood and left the room with Mrs Wolden's hand on my shoulder.

As she guided me to Principal Dahl's office, I imagined the expulsion ahead. *"Mr Spooner, we know things haven't been good at home, but that's no excuse for abusing another student. You strangled him! That kind of behaviour won't be tolerated here at St Bridget's. What on earth has got into you? You used to be a good guy. 'Considerate and talented, but over-anxious'—that's what your report cards said. You used to be* you. *Don't you miss that person?"* What would I tell my mother once the news reached her, considering everything else going on? She'd almost looked fearful of me (not for me) when I asked about the woman with the long red hair that morning. Because how could I have known unless I'd betrayed her. The way she searched my face when the tree came through the wall, seeking out my part to play in all of this. My culpability in the crime. Maybe Dad wasn't with the red-haired woman. Maybe his disappearance had something to do with whatever was going on with me. That dark, dirty magic that had come from nowhere, like the fingertip of a great hand shooting out of the sky to get me.

*You. Not anyone else. You.*

And worse, maybe she knew it.

*Give me the thunder,* I thought. *Shake the room. Crack the windows. Make things normal again.*

Crucifixes lined the walls of Principal Dahl's office. Dusty trophies etched with names. The room echoed with the wicker-crack of past canings, though the cane was retired by the time I went through school. The smell of Old Spice and sweat.

Mrs Wolden closed the door, abandoning me in the dim room with Dahl and another teacher, Scabs, dubbed so by students after the hardened skin on both his knees (never-healing wounds he dressed with pink peroxide). Guys said he got them from giving blowjobs. Dahl and Scabs towered over Brett Oldfield, who was hunched in a chair. He seemed so small. My hands linked as though defaulting to prayer. Our teachers, burly men with beards and the prickle-blemish of too many beers, wore knee-high socks.

They forced Brett to apologise.

"Calling someone that word is truly despicable," Scabs said.

"There's nothing more un-Christian," said Dahl. "It's the deepest offence there is." He put his slightly too long nails to his lips. Eyes shimmered and I thought again of the ants escaping the drain in the boy's bathroom, spiralling up and out.

Brett mumbled a few words. Whatever he said was enough for me.

Not for these men, though.

I wished for the courage to stand up to them and say it takes hatred to make a word hateful, and that Brett didn't have hate in him—not really. Only fear. He'd called me a faggot because the assault was easy. *It's* you *guys who have that hate.* Looking down at my pathetic bully, I realised I didn't hate him. Brett wasn't that different from me. I should have told Dahl and Scabs there were more despicable things than stupid fear tossed across a quadrangle. Things like institutionalised homophobia. The presumption of evil in the eyes of adults who have lived long enough to know better. Why use canes to whip the young when you've got doctrine to do it for you? It wasn't hard to see the two teachers in dark cloaks, scythes in one hand and bowling balls in the other, dry ice billowing around their ankles.

"Brett," Principal Dahl said, settling his hands on the desk. "You're expelled."

———————————————————————————

Though my body moved along the path, a clockwork plaything in the shape of a boy, my thoughts remained in Dahl's office, watching Brett's head fall again and again in a kind of video loop. Up to down. Glitch. Up to down. Glitch. Static. Dirty heads in need of cleaning. Sounds slipped through the hiss. The way the plaything's shoes crunched dry grass. Swishing backpack against a sweaty shirt. And whatever it was Dee said. She grew impatient and pushed me, turning wood and plastic to flesh again.

"Why are you ignoring me?" she said. "I hate that."

If there was an apology in me, the apology was lost. I pushed on, one foot at a time. We passed houses, some with empty Saxby milk crates still out front, coated in grit, waiting for a pickup and subsequent delivery that wouldn't come on time. Wind blew over those empty bottles, filling the street with a ghostly *ooooohhhh*. Quiet forced my sister to speak. Dee never was good with awkward silences.

"Do you think Mum has gone to the police again?" she said.

A shrug of the shoulders was all I had to give.

"Earth to Heath? Hello—"

"Yeah, Dee," I snapped, harsher than intended. "Reckon she has."

We walked side-by-side, following our shadows that trailed ahead as if trying to escape us. *Can't blame them. We're bad news. We're cursed.* I thought of Peter Pan and how he tried to re-attach his darker self with soap. Given the chance, I'd let my shadow go. I'd rather be incomplete than rob a part of me the chance to be free of this pain. Especially when I was the kind of person who strangled others. Who *hissed*.

"What if Dad's hurt?" she said.

"Look, we've got to stop thinking that way, Dee. This is all doing my head in."

"Can't you just pretend to care?"

"Of course, I care," I said, stopping. "Don't say that."

"You sure got a funny way of showing it, if you do." Dee stared me down. She looked older than she was. The ghost cry droned on. She sighed, readjusting her bag and asked, "Do you think Dad's got Penny with him?"

"No," I said. "I don't think he does."

Dee kicked a rock at her feet. "I guess I don't think that, either." I hated seeing her back to me. A rush of guilt.

"I'm sorry," I said. "I'm—I'm being a total dick."

"You said it, not me."

"I'm saying it for the both of us then. It's been a really bad day."

Understatement of the year, or maybe my life. The words were false and cheap in my mouth, and my body rejected them. Shakes made my knees buckle. Stopping the tears proved impossible. I buried my face in the crook of my elbow and hoped Dee would run off so she wouldn't see me this weak. She was still there when I let my arm drop, my cheeks wet—sunshine steamed them quick.

"It's going to be okay," she said. Her voice sounded tiny. "Please don't cry. That'll make *me* cry."

Dee drew close and bopped her hip against mine. It shocked me how tall she'd gotten. "I won't tell anyone you're upset," she said. "Our secret."

I didn't want to laugh but laughed anyway, snot bubbles popping. Her consideration mattered. I bopped her hip back.

"Let's go," she said. "Mum and Aunt Kat need us."

Beat. The ghosts kept howling. Red country dust swirled between us.

"Dee?" I said, wiping my nose.

"What, shit for brains?"

"Look at you swearing! It doesn't make you any cooler," I said, mimicking her. It made Dee smile, and that smile made me feel like not all hope was lost. "Dee…"

She raised her eyebrows, telling me it was okay to continue. If I wanted to.

"Dee…" My throat was thick. "Dee, I'm worried I'm…"

(*Say it,* said a voice deep inside me. *Say the word.*)

"I'm…"

(*Gay.*)

"…that I'm different."

Dee sighed, though the sigh was kind. She tilted her head to the sun, peach fuzz on her cheeks and neck glowing. Beads of sweat along her upper lip caught the light like glitter. She looked at me, looked at me deeply, and in that look, I saw my parents. Only there was compassion in her face they never awarded us, and maybe weren't designed to.

"I know," she said. "And I don't care."

Dee gestured at the road ahead and waited for me to join her. We didn't speak the rest of the way, passing our **LOST** posters, breadcrumbs leading us back to Mason Drive.

Dad's van was still in the driveway, the aunty-mobile behind it. Before heading in, we confided in each other about how terrified we were. This we said without having to use our mouths. I swelled with love for my sister and the woman I wanted to watch her grow into, looking forward to the day when this was behind us, when we were older, and not just siblings. When we were friends. All this, and more, I told her. But only with my eyes.

I pulled the front door open. The stink of bleach hit us hard.

---

Mum and Aunt Kat huddled at the kitchen table, silhouetted by windows overlooking the yard where sheets and pillowcases billowed on the clothesline, from the backs of chairs and a sawhorse. Instead of stewing in misery, these women had twisted anxiety into chores, resulting in a cleaning spree. Even the stove door, normally dense with grease, had been scrubbed. A celebratory bottle of gin sat within reach of my mother. It was half empty.

Aunt Kat watched us enter, breaking out in a smile.

"Come here, kids," Mum said, arms opening. "What a day." Hugs and an alcohol fog. My understanding of booze was limited, but I always thought it was a night-time thing. "I want you both to know the missing person's report has been filed," she told us. "Got to be strong now." Mum touched Dee's cheek and dropped her hand to the table a tad too hard, her wedding ring rapping the wood. All I wanted to do was tell her something terrible was happening to me and that Dad's ring was in the field behind school. I didn't—too afraid she'd hate me, if she didn't hate me already. Because how couldn't you hate something so unnatural? Later, I promised myself, I'd pinch the skin beneath the hem of my shorts again.

Aunt Kat spoke up. "You'll be seeing a bit more of me for a while, too. Until things settle and your father's back. How's that sound?"

"Choice," I said, meaning it even if it sounded like I didn't. Aunt Kat brought warmth with her wherever she went. It had never been more welcome. "So, what next?"

Mum slurred her words, caught the slur, tried to rein it in. "We've been given a case worker. The go-between. I told her everything. Dad isn't at the hospital. And starting tomorrow there's going to be a search. Door knocking. Searching the bush around here, like in one of your movies, Heath. There will be a press conference thingy after school." A frown creased her brow. "To—to, um, raise awareness." She touched her forehead.

Dee started to cry. "I knew this would happen," she said.

My pulse rattled. I wanted to comfort my sister, but Aunt Kat picked up her cane and led her from the room, whispering *there, there.* Mum remained in her seat, raising her glass to me. Her teeth clipped the rim as she sipped. I thought she was about to chew it and swallow the pieces, bleeding herself dry from the inside out, as I screamed, watching, unable to do anything, because whatever course we were on couldn't be corrected. We'd all gone too far. She just closed her eyes instead. I did nothing because nothing, staying still, was safer.

―――――――――――――――――――――――

Television occupied our silence in the living room, drowning out evening crickets, that lonely summer drone. My attention kept drifting to the staircase, to the door up at the end of the hall. Darkness there. I still wasn't allowed to go to my room yet. Tomorrow, maybe, Mum had told me. After the landlords had come by and seen what couldn't be there. But was.

*The Simpsons* came on once the news reports wrapped. Not so long ago, that cartoon meant everything to me. Mustering a giggle was impossible now.

Aunt Kat and Dee reclined on the couch, hugging pillows. Mum remained at the kitchen table with her drink and documents the police had left for her. Sighs wafted to where I laid in my shorts and singlet top on the shag rug, trying to draw. The pencil hovered above the blank page, as I knew it would. Maybe I should've gone to the basement. No point. The well was empty. The strange lightning from earlier had evaporated every drop of inspiration in me. Still, I waited for thunder.

*Empty. Empty. Empty.*

My stomach repeated the word with muscles and juices. Dinner was on the stove, the meat-stink a maddening prod. I got up every now and then to stir the pot. Salivating, I licked the spoon. Sucked the wood. Spooner Bolognaise.

*Empty. Empty. Empty. EMPTY.*

The upright fan shifted from left to right, right to left. Mum had draped a wet towel over it again in the hopes of cooling the living room for us. It wasn't working. Summer always won. I went back to the blank page, which was also charmless.

Ice clinked within Mum's glass.

An occasional cough from Dee.

Dogs barked in the neighbourhood.

The phone rang and Dee jumped off the couch. Mum stood so fast her chair overturned. "DON'T ANSWER IT!" My sister froze, deer in headlights, hand poised above the receiver as the tinny bell cried. Mum stormed into the living room, saying, "You don't know who it might be."

"No need to talk to her like that," Aunt Kat said, standing to pin back her long silver hair. "Dee didn't do this to us."

Mum exhaled and snatched the phone with both hands. The spiral cord hung in a smile. "Hello?" Her voice was a whisper, nothing more.

Out of the blue, I wondered what it would be like to never see my father again, all those photos on the memory wall the last ever taken.

Mum pushed the receiver in our direction. "Heath, it's Lincoln." Disappointment and relief sounded one and the same.

The last thing I wanted was to talk to anyone, yet I found myself getting up anyway. Mum avoided eye contact as I took the phone. "Hey, Lincoln," I said, turning to face the wall. Eyes burrowed into me from behind.

"Where were you today, Spoons? I was worried about—"

His voice bleached away. My focus shifted to my mother, feet wisping over the living room carpet, as she strolled into her bedroom. She returned with an empty laundry basket. Walked right by me. The rear door to the backyard opened, slammed. Tension thickened. Sauce bubbled on the stovetop. Spluttered. I needed it soon or I'd die. *Empty*, went my stomach again. *Empty. Empty. EMPTY. EMPTY!*

"Can I buzz you later, Lincoln?"

"Sure, Spoons. You okay? I could—"

Hanging up on my best friend without saying goodbye would be something I'd play over in my head for years to come, a loop from the worst movie that ever was, intercut with scenes of monsters and exploding fruit. Lincoln deserved better than that. He really did.

Dee returned to Aunt Kat's side on the couch. *The Simpsons* gave way to a commercial for Sealy Posturepedic in which a mother and father in bright clothes tossed a blanket across their brand-new bed, but not before kids with smiles like bone-white scars dove onto the mattress. So cheeky. So happy. So keen to wake up on top of the world, and on top of a Posturepedic.

"Jesus *fucking* Christ," Mum shouted from outside.

I ran through the kitchen—past the pot, the bottle of gin— to the back door. Threw it open. Stepped into the new night, jasmine heavy on the air.

Sheets glowed blue in the moonlight. The laundry basket lay on its side at Mum's feet. She held her head, hair blooming through her fingers. I drew near, weaving around chairs and A-frames as crickets chimed in waves, surging and dipping.

"What happened, Mum?"

"Goddamned birds have gone and shit over everything."

Aunt Kat tapped over the threshold behind me. "Stay inside, Dee," I heard her say.

"What's going on?" Dee shouted. "Nobody tells me fuck 'round this place!"

"Dee Spooner! I might be your aunt, but I'll wash your mouth out with soap lickedy-split if you continue speaking that way."

"Mum, let me help you. Let's—" Only I didn't get a chance to finish my offer. She ran to the clothesline and ripped a soiled sheet off the wire, pegs pin-wheeling. "Fucking things! God damn fucking fucks." Each curse was a whiplash. Everything strong in her turned feral and worn. In that moment, I hated Dad as much as I hated myself for bringing this toxicity into our family. Dad, and whatever else was happening.

*The dark magic—because what else could it be? It dragged a tree through my wall. The tape in the tree that I'd buried. Something is sick in this house. Don't deny it. It's turning us, and especially Mum, into someone she's not. Dark magic. Just because it came from nowhere doesn't mean it doesn't exist. And you're a part of it, Spoons. You know it.*

Aunt Kat went to her sister and attempted to pry the sheets from her hands. "Stop this now, sweetheart."

"I've had it, Kat," Mum said.

"Give me this stuff. I can take care of it."

"Let go," she snapped. "It's *mine.* You don't understand what it's like, Kat. Nobody does."

This had nothing to do with the sheets.

Their sisterhood couldn't be mistaken. I'd never imagined them as kids before. Why would I? They were old. Now they fought over nothing and everything, just like Dee and I. *Old.* All the oldness in the Milky Way.

"Fuck it," Mum said, turning away. "I'm going."

"Don't be daft," Aunt Kat said. She faced me. "Heath, go to your sister."

I half stepped backwards. Stilled.

"I mean it," Mum went on, facing Kat again. "I'm going over there right now. I need to know. I bet my bottom dollar the bitch saw him before he buggered off."

Guilt beamed through me. I never should have spoken about the woman with the red hair. I certainly shouldn't have dreamed about her, either—even if it hadn't been my dream to begin with. Somehow, somehow so strangely, Dad's secrets were *inside* me now. The secret of the woman he'd been cheating on my mother with, and how he took off his wedding ring when he went to her house to fuck her.

*Is Dad* hungry *wherever he is right now?*
*Does that explain why my stomach hurts?*
*Or does that hunger come from something else?*

"You're torturing yourself," Kat said to my mother. "Come inside. Let's ease off the grog for a bit and have tea instead, and—"

"I said, no." Mum kicked the basket and walked' past me, caressing my shoulder as she went, a diminutive gesture I didn't know how badly I needed until it was given. *You're not unimportant here*, it said. *You still count. But you'll count more later. Once I'm through.* "Nobody'll stop me."

Kat limped after her sister. I stepped out of the way and watched them scuttle into the house. "Don't think for one second you're driving the car," my aunt yelled, voice echoing through the kitchen window and out to where I remained on the lawn. I watched them through the window. "There's not a snowball's chance in hell I'm lettin' you go over to that woman's house to make a fool of yourself on your own. I'm coming with you. Oh, put the keys down, you buffoon. Dad wrapped his car around a tree, drunk as a skunk. Are you going to run off and kill yourself, too? Are you that adamant to make orphans of your beautiful children? Set the right example and drop those keys right now. Good. Good! And now, for the love of God, chew a bloody mint or brush your teeth. You reek of the brewery, just like Mum did."

Aunt Kat emerged from the back door, leaning on her cane, wheezing as she always wheezed, face sheened with sweat. "Heath, sweet dove. Your mother's gone off half-cocked, as you've no doubt heard. I'm going with her. We'll need you to keep an eye on your sister while we're out."

"You're not driving, are you?" I said. It was a bit of a power play. I knew she'd been drinking, too.

"Heavens, no. My knees'll be killin' by the time we get back, but we're off on foot."

"Where to?" I said, even though I knew. "It's late—"

"Just adult stuff, Heath. I need you to be a good big brother and stay put. We'll be back sooner rather than later if I've got sway in the matter, believe-you-me."

The door clapped shut. I could hear Dee asking if she could go with them, followed by a chorus of nos. Silence descended over the yard. Sheets wafted as the surrounding trees moaned bark against bark in the wind. A bird landed on the fence separating our yard from the adjoining property, letting loose a Disney-style *cheep* before flying off, crossing the quarter moon. Throughout it all, the wave of crickets broke on a shore I hardly recognised any more.

"Heath?" said my sister, almost in panic. "Where are you?"

Tears skidded my cheeks. I backhanded them away before slipping inside, stopping to take in the yard, a ghostly lot of laundry I'd dismantle and bring in later. One less thing for Mum to worry about when she got home. The lemon tree lurked in the corner, so willow thin. And dead.

# FIVE

Earlier that morning, before enduring the awfulness of school, the morning of what I'd come to think of as the last day, Mum made it clear to the boy I used to be and that boy's sister that they wouldn't be sleeping in their rooms until the landlords gave everyone the 'all clear'.

"What are you expecting them to do?" I'd said, schoolbag hanging off my shoulder. "They're not *ghost* gardeners." My half joke about the mysterious tree was only half as clever as I thought, and my mother, never one to indulge in smarm, led me to the cot in her room that she'd made up, and pointed at the floor.

Answer enough. We smiled at each other. And that final smile was good.

Memories are shards. This is a shard of the woman I knew. Were it not for the photograph of her I keep in my backpack with the Salvation Army cans with no labels and the stuff I've stolen from malls across the state, I'm worried I wouldn't remember how she looked. Things you thought were unforgettable slip away. You don't get over loss like that. You just get better at dealing with it. That and more, I've learned sleeping rough.

Maybe that's why I came back to Townsend Heights. Not to defeat the shadow with too many teeth, my monster. But to let these shards go for good.

# FOUR

9pm edged closer but I wasn't in the neighbourhood of sleepy. My sister on the other hand, had sprawled on the couch and nodded off in front of a *Roseanne* re-run. Mismatched dinner plates rested on the coffee table between us, their surfaces illustrated in sauce smiles. I'd wash them up soon. Mum hated it when we left the dishes for the following morning, called it 'common'. Heady meat smells in our townhouse where it always felt hotter inside than outside. I could've eaten more of our dinner despite having already had two helpings. My stomach kept crying, moaning.

The tub chair gave a wheeze as I hopped onto it feet-first (naughty!). A supposedly real audience laughed on the program. There was nothing there I found funny. I stared through the screen at my reflection in the glass instead.

What was the genre of the movie of my life, I wondered? There had been a time—not so long ago—when I would've referred to it as something G-Rated. Sure, things had never been upscale Amblin like they were at the Leoungs', but we Spooners were comfy in our little lives in our little house with our little dramas, us kids chasing little adventures on little bikes. The VHS of *that* life would be in the **FAMILY** section at Top Video Universe, an aisle I rarely visited yet found weird comfort in when I did.

Everything was different now.

Important pieces had been spliced out of that movie. And the empty spaces took the shape of those we loved. Dad. Our cat, Penny. Maybe that's why Stacy with the nose-ring would stock the video of my life in the **MYSTERY** section.

*Come on, Spoons. Have you forgotten about the tree in your wall? The feeling that everything's about to go wrong?*

"No, Stacy," I would tell her. "I haven't. Come to think of it, maybe I don't belong in the **MYSTERY** section after all. Try **HORROR**."

The movie of my life would be rated R because my life was dirty. It featured a seed snatched from my head and planted in a wall. Green ants where there shouldn't be green ants. Lightning with no thunder. The impossible versus the impossible to deny.

This movie was about magic. So, who was the magician?

Possible answers crushed the question. Listening to Dee's snores, the rhythmic in and out, a whistle in her nose, helped distract me. Her hand dangled over the side of the couch, twitching. *Dreaming*, I figured. *I hope wherever she is now is better than here.* My eyes drifted to the clock on the wall beside wooden ornamental birds flying in V formation. And then to the staircase, which led to darkness where we weren't allowed to go.

*Tick-tock. Tick-tock.*

Mosquitoes buzzed by my ears when I stepped outside to look up and down the street, as if just being out there would conjure my father. It didn't work. Moths clouded the streetlamps, making shadow static in the pools of light where Saxby bottles waited to be picked up. My father's work van was by my side. I put my head to the dusty glass and stared in at the hub. Dark logbooks against dark seats. A dark toolkit against a dark floor.

Dark.

The darkness didn't last. Memory grabbed me—only it wasn't my memory.

I'm behind the wheel. I'm grabbing the toolkit with my big, calloused hands. Filling the logbook to ensure I'm compensated for fuel. I drive down Mason Drive, sunlight through the trees, sputtering glare on my face like splashes of hot grease. Wilson Phillips on the radio. Turning it off. Hate that shit. Quiet after the chaos of the morning rush at home with the kids banging on and on and—

I lifted my head from the window, startled. The darkness of the street was deeper than it had been a moment before. My eyes must have closed at some point to let the fantasy play out, a crossed reception from another movie fighting for airtime. Dad's movie. It had been filmed the morning he left us, when he forgot his lunch and Dee chased after him but hadn't chased quick enough. The last time I saw him.

*"Be goooood," he'd said in his best E.T. impersonation, walking backwards into the living room with his index finger raised. Car keys clattered. The clank of the screen door slapping. And how his van roared to life, the sound fading as he drove away.*

My heart felt like rocks in a tin can. I could have sworn that warmth of the sun through the trees had been on *my* face. That it had been *me* inside the vehicle inhaling the newspapery mustiness. Grit beneath my work boots as I accelerated to work, or maybe not to work at all. Maybe I (he) had been going to her.

*She stares with jade green eyes. "When do you think you'll leave your wife?"*

Another mosquito buzzed by my ear. Disorientated, afraid, I went back into our home, closing the door behind me. I kept it unlocked for Mum and Aunt Kat. Keeping my fingers off the deadbolt was a challenge. I wanted to lock out whatever magic was closing in on me, all the things I couldn't explain away, all the things that had been creeping up on me since that day at The Truck Graveyard. My discovery of Clayton McManus, the man I didn't just want to be like someday. The man I—

*(say it, Heath)*

—wanted. That I desired.

Locks were not going to keep me safe.

I splayed my hands against the door and pushed. Anger coursed through me.

*How dare he,* I thought? *Why would Dad do this to Mum? Doesn't he love us any more? When I grow up and get married, I'll never—*

My hands dropped, that energy spent. Laughter from the television filled my ears as I slouched to the staircase railing, a depression so thick it curdled the air, made it heavy and difficult to pass through, overcoming me. I saw the photos in the frames, settling on those from Mum and Dad's wedding. Her white dress looked so beautiful, the dress Dee wanted handed down to her when the time was right. And Dad, so skinny but handsome with his wide—almost too wide—smile. It dawned on me then that unless things changed, I would never have what they had because gay people weren't allowed to get married. Gay people caught AIDS and then the Grim Reaper with his scythe and bowling ball came prowling. Gay people weren't allowed to say who they were at work. Secret lives for secret people. What was sex supposed to be then? How was I ever supposed to touch myself without feeling shame? There weren't videos in the adult section behind the beaded curtain, surely, for people like me. I'd hate for Stacy or Brennan to find out. That would kill me. What would Dahl and Scabs say? What about everyone at school? What about Lincoln? Gay people, the fags, the poofs, the weak men and the weak women and the weak people who didn't fit into either box, lived lonely lives. Because how could they not be lonely when they all must feel the way I felt, as if they had been abandoned against their will with all maps erased. What was happiness when people you didn't even know hated you? Where did you fit in? Why do you exist? So, maybe, you shouldn't exist.

Maybe *I* shouldn't exist.

There was danger at the top of the stairs—that I felt in my bones. And I quietly took the first step without having to think twice, and then another, and another again, every impulse drawing me towards that danger, because in danger there was a way out. Risk might kill me. And that was okay.

Stairs groaned as I inched higher. Sound distorted, that ticking clock on the wall, the laughter of the television audience, the upright fan. Everything stretched into white noise. Sweat beaded my brow. It was hotter here on the landing, bathroom on the left and our closed bedrooms ahead. A headache crawled in my skull, a living thing, something that hunted for my eyes and wanted to eat them from the inside out.

I stepped to where the shadows were thickest.

The doorhandle clicked, hinges a bored choir at school. Moonlight scrubbed everything blue—the blue bed, blue posters on blue walls. *Come closer*, crooned the blue. That voice was saccharine and spineless, chocolate extended from a stranger's van.

Still, I answered it. Took the chocolate. Took the bait.

I fingered the stump where the lemon tree had been. At some point during the day, either Mum or Aunt Kat had taken a saw to it. Three inches of wood remained. Shavings dusted the floorboards between my toes.

A sigh of disappointment, a climax robbed, wriggled out from between my lips. The air thickened again as if in response. Everything turned heavy. There was no dangerous magic in my room after all. Head lowered, I shuffled out into the hall, forced to continue existing, uncertain as to if that was a good or bad thing. And stopped.

Light shifted behind me. I turned back to see my room bruise from dim to dark as clouds strangled the moon. Every joint in my body ached, guts knotting. The posters on either side of the tree stump shivered as though a draft had climbed between the paper and the wall—which didn't make sense because the window was shut.

"Hello?"

Nobody answered.

A movie poster beside the stump bulged far enough to cast its own shadow. The horror actress shifted her suspicious eyes to meet mine. I snatched my throat, shocked. This wasn't my imagination playing tricks. Blu-Tack pried free of the wall and the shadow of her profile cast over the floorboards, mouth opening wide. The poster slammed the ground, the thud implying a heaviness that outweighed what rightly should be there.

*Don't scream, Heath! Don't be* weak.

The next poster swelled, too, the image of a bloodied hand starting to flex. It grew from two-dimensions into three, and also thudded against the floorboards. I jumped at that '*Hello, is anyone home*' knock of knuckles on wood. Knuckles that shouldn't exits, but which did exist. There in the room. The danger room. The dirty room belonging to the dirty boy.

Blisters flowered in the blue paint my parents had—before my birth—lathered the room with as something shifted behind the wall. Something hot. I heard footsteps in the townhouse next door and thought:

*Holy shit. We're not alone. Someone's over there.*

Paint flakes drifted and rained down from above, the room a snow globe in a souvenir shop. I had one tucked away somewhere from a class snow trip in the sixth grade. Lincoln and I had shared a seat in the cramped bus on the way down, which the driver had to pull over every now and then for a carsick student to vomit out the window, later sharing a room in a bunk bed with other boys who got us into trouble for laughing too loudly after lights out. That memory, like the snow globe I brought home to show my parents, seemed so very far away. Irrelevant. The memory of someone who no longer existed, who maybe never had.

The lurker retreated. I could hear their feet shuffling behind the wall we shared with the empty townhouse.

Posters squirmed on the ground, just-born things that didn't know how to walk. Disbelief ushered me into the hall. Something banged in the adjoining property again, a sound I could almost follow with the precision of Superman's X-Ray vision.

I followed its descent, only on my side of the wall, thinking as I went: *My posters are alive. The wall is melting. And I know, earlier, outside, that I saw my father's hands gripping the wheel of his van. No more denying. No more.*

After thumping down the staircase, I skidded into the kitchen. Dee shifted on the couch in the living room behind me, letting loose a moan. It was getting harder to breathe, but instinct told me to push on, that whoever was next door, like me, was descending. Down as far as they could go.

———————————————————————————————

My van turns onto another street. Trees peel back. The sun, a bright, unblinking eye in the sky watching me. I roll down the window to let the fresh air in. I can hardly breathe in this shitty old vehicle, damn it.

———————————————————————————————

*BREATHE.*

It's wicked how fast your body betrays you. I wasn't breathing, even though I knew I needed to. Fear jammed out oxygen from entering my system, knot in a drinking straw. Asthma wasn't something I had to worry about, unlike other kids in my year who never ventured far without an inhaler. But I shared their betrayal now. This was *my* body. *Mine. Give it back. Obey me. Do as I say.*

*Do it now.*

BREATHE.

*Because if you don't, you'll die. You know what death is. Death is what happened to Nana Spooner. Do you want to end up in a coffin with the lid closed so you don't make other people cry? And once the funeral is over, they'll bury you, food for the worms. You know what worms do. They eat your eyes. If that happens, you won't have to worry about the Grim Reaper with his scythe and bowling ball, Heath. You won't have to worry about anything.*

I flung the basement door open, my lips opening. Air whistled into my system through gritted teeth.

Kitchen light stretched only so far. If I did what I thought I was about to do, and went down there, I'd be stumbling through the semi-dark until reaching the drawstring bulb in the middle of the room. The concept made me sick.

*Don't do it, Spoons,* chimed Lincoln's echo.

*Do it and you're dead meat,* hissed Brett Oldfield. *Cruisin' for a bruisin'.*

*Help me,* said my father. *Save me, Heath.*

Dad emerged in my imagination like unfolding origami,

features sketched in 2HB pencil. *Show me how to be brave*, I asked this phantom. *Show me how to get down these steps and protect us from whatever's happening, Dad. You're my old man and it's your job to do this. Show me what bravery looks like. This is our family. Don't abandon us now.*

The paper man didn't move. He stared with cartoon eyes. It couldn't show me what I needed to see because Dad never showed it to me in real life. He'd sooner hide behind a book, one of those volumes from the top shelf that we weren't allowed to touch, smiling instead of saying it was okay to be alarmed. He rarely challenged me because affirmations were easy. He wasn't the kind of guy to point out role models for fear it made him appear lesser, as though there could only be so much heroism in the world at any one given time.

The paper figure folded in on itself and re-bloomed as my mother. These drawn-on eyes were sterner, but fairer. Here stood the person who pulled me into line when I needed correcting, who pushed me into the deep end where I didn't want to go because she knew I had to figure out how to swim.

Who was she, really?

Who was the woman behind the image I held of her? The one who kept our family going, giving lessons along the way without us even realising it?

Even though I'd aged over the past endless week, I was still a child. A boy who wanted to be a man. That wouldn't always be the case, hopefully. Standing there at the threshold to the dark basement, I hungered for the opportunity to meet my mother as equals. This would occur when the time was right, when I could see who she really was. And when I was brave enough to tell her who I was, too.

Something changed in me then. Not ten minutes earlier, I'd crept upstairs into the dark because the risk of dying seemed tempting, an easy way out. Now, as I rushed into the darkness below, I hoped for light. The change was swift and caught me off guard. But there was no mistaking it. Yes, there it was.

Hope.

The stairs gave way to concrete underfoot. I noticed the light tab up ahead, glimmering like a tooth. Grabbed it. Yanked the cord. The whale's mouth of the basement where I came to draw my monsters refused to reveal itself. Because the bulb wasn't there.

Gasping, I scanned the dark room for something—anything—that didn't belong.

And to my surprise, found it.

The washing machine wasn't aligned against the wall quite right. Even in the limited light from upstairs, I could see scratches in the cement that implied it had been moved forward and then shuffled back. I dropped to my knees, the old Band Aids peeling off, to trace the divots with my fingernails.

A bitter smell like something at the bottom of your schoolbag when you forget to unpack your leftovers, rotting food, reached me. I slid onto my side, breath blowing a plume of dust, and peered under the shelves to my left. Sweat I wasn't even aware I was shedding, beaded into my eye. Stung. Blink. Focused. Strained to see.

An apple rotted amongst the rubble of plaster, its sticker peering from blackened skin.

The memory came on strong.

We were all in the kitchen on the morning of Dad's disappearance, the radio playing Michael Jackson's *Black or White*. I remembered wishing it had come on the night before so I could have recorded it to Tina's mixtape. Mum sung along, getting the lyrics wrong, handing me an apple from the fridge to put in my father's paper lunch bag on the ironing board. I remembered the firmness of its peel under my grip. How white my fingers appeared against that deep red. How the bag crunched. My assumption that I'd see my father again later when I got home from school. Why wouldn't I think that? Bad things don't happen to people like us. We were normal. We were us.

# THREE

"We shouldn't be here," Dee said. "We're going to be in deep trouble."

*Deep trouble.* The way she said it sounded motherly. The echo of a parental threat now the shape of a child's worry. Dee used it against me, her threat directed at me now. Falling dominoes in a row I had no choice but to push back against.

"Would you just help me, okay?"

"Please don't make me do this, Heath."

I turned to her, biting my thumbnail. "I can't tell you how I know this, but Dad was down here for some reason," I said. "The police, Mum, Aunt Kat, they haven't seen what I've seen. There's something going on here. Something weird."

"Stop talking this way," she said. "You're scaring me. I'm going upstairs—"

"No! We need to help him." I puffed out my chest, dropping my arms, the skin around my thumbnail bloody from where I'd nibbled too far. I was The Big Brother. The one who was in charge when we were left alone at Top Video Universe. "Dad's still with us." Exhale. "I think."

"Whatch'ya mean?"

The headache, which had been plaguing me for so long, worsened. Everything throbbed along with my pulse, expanding and then constricting. "This is our job, Dee," I said, trying to control the pain instead of it controlling me. "We're his kids. He wasn't perfect but we've got to help him. Who's going to do it if we don't? Nobody would believe me if I told them what I've seen. Something—something is upstairs. It's—I can't describe it. Dee, I'm not even that scared, come to think of it. Because, well, I feel kind of…"

Dee waited for me to speak, hanging off every word. "You feel what?" Her voice had a ring of challenge to it. She softened, realising how serious things had become. "Tell me."

I glanced away, shamed. "I feel connected to it."

Thoughts zoomed to the mixtape's re-emergence in the lemon tree, how the tape fluttered when I ripped it from the branches and shoved it under the bed. Hungry ants as they spiralled out of the drain. Lightning in the field and the thunder that didn't follow. Posters for films I held in high regard even though I'd never seen them, coming alive, faces filling with flesh. These events weren't accidents, but consequences. Welts on an infection, on a wrongness. They were my scabs. My blisters. My sickness oozing free and changing the world, mutations I couldn't hate or fear because they were a part of me.

"My fault," I said. "This is all my fault."

"What are you even talking about?" *Expanding and then constricting.* "Heath?" *Expanding and then constricting.* "Heath, are you okay?"

Sunshine on my cheeks again.

---

I stop the van in front of a house with alfoil pinwheels in its yard. Kill the engine. Listen to the tick-tick-tick of the fan belt, an anticipatory sound. Keys dangle from the ignition, touching my knee. Metal against ultra-sensitive skin. I step into the day, surrounded by houses. My steel-capped work boots clunk against the driveway. Morning wind blows those pinwheels, turning the veranda into a kaleidoscope of spinning colours. I pass a crate of empty Saxby bottles I'll take with me once I'm done here.

The front door opens.

A slender hand snatches at the shirt my wife ironed.

This woman's fingernail catches on my nipple. It feels amazing. Her red hair knits over my vision, blinding me in the best possible way.

---

"Heath?" Dee said, kneeling to hold me. I flinched. "Don't do that." She smacked my upper arm. "You're wigging me out."

"W-what?" There was a ringing in my ears.

"You're acting creepy. You're doing it on purpose."

"Hungry," I said. "I'm so hungry."

"Then let's go back upstairs and eat," she pleaded, almost at the point of tears. "I'll make you something. Mum says I'm good at cooking." She rationalised for the both of us. "Sandwiches. We've got Vegemite. I'll cut the crusts off." Dee glanced around the basement. "You like the crusts cut off, don't you? I'm good at it. I'm good at it, Heath."

Moments were greasy things I couldn't grasp, leaving no time to process what I'd seen—or experienced. *Shake it off,* I tried to command of myself. *You've got to.* But the vision of the woman with the red hair was a web. I sensed the spider at the middle of it edging closer.

"Help me." My voice broke to bleed the emotion out. I don't know who I was even speaking to. "It was bright. I'm so hungry."

My little sister tilted her head back, mustering nerve. I watched her cool. "What do you need me to do?" she said, resigned to her part to play in whatever plan I was building blind. Her words were a buoy I clung to. I promised myself to make this up to her once all this bullshit was behind us and our family reunited, normality—or whatever normality was to us—restored. I took Dee by the shoulder, forcing her towards the washing machine. We stood side-by-side.

"It's been moved," Dee said, pointing at the scratches.

"Then moved back, see. A few times maybe."

"And you think Dad did this? Why?"

"Just grab this corner," I said, avoiding the question. "I'll grab the other."

The old Fisher & Paykel top-loader weighed more than anticipated. That didn't stop us, though. We Spooner kids heaved, we pushed, fingers slipping but holding true. We had to. We were committed to this now. The metal edge rubbed the well-worn concrete, issuing a nails-on-a-chalkboard screech that ricocheted through the basement.

A yard-wide hole in the wall was revealed.

"Holy shit," I said.

"Holy shit," Dee echoed—meaning it but also testing me, in a way asking if she'd earned the curse. I nodded, and she didn't gloat. Because it meant something to her to receive that validation from me. Shock bonded us. We were siblings, yes. But now we were siblings with a mission.

This wasn't *just* a hole through plaster and tile and asbestos, fat-yellow insulation dripping like cobwebs. It was an entry/exit point big enough for a man to squeeze through if he was desperate enough. And it wasn't the work of a hammer or pick, either. These looked like claw marks, like something had tic-tac-toed its way between the two properties.

*Cat claws,* I thought.

I rested my hand on the shelf above the vacated space, knocking the wood off its sprockets. The paling clattered to my side and the box of powdered detergent I'd brought downstairs after our last Kellyville trip sailed through the air. It struck the floor, busted open, spraying granules over our sweaty shins, sticking there.

Then: Placing the detergent on the shelf.

Now: Knocking the detergent to the floor.

These were the mundane bookends to the worst days of my life.

I peered through the hole.

"Don't," Dee whispered.

"Why would Dad hide over there?" I said.

"How do you know he did this?"

"It *was* him, Dee," I said, confident. "I feel it."

*Find him,* whispered the origami version of my mother. *Piece us back together.*

Rocks stabbed the undersides of my feet as I twisted around, shoulders straining, perpendicular to the wall. The scratch marks were threatening.

The force it must have taken. The patience.

"Over on that shelf," I said to my sister, gesturing to the other side of the basement with my chin. "There's a torch. Pretty sure I saw it the other day. Grab it for me, will ya?"

Dee did as I asked and came back, piggie-print socks shuffling over the concrete I used to draw on for hours on end. Ours was the kind of household where no remote or toy or transistor wireless was fully charged when you needed it to be. Battery 'musical chairs'. But on that hot summer's night, the torch in the yellow casing she handed over worked fine. A shaft of light lanced the dusty basement when I clicked the rubber button.

My sister asked me to be careful. She asked me with her eyes. I didn't answer. She knew I'd try, which was why she let me go.

The jagged teeth of the hole grazed the back of my thighs and across my buttocks as I lifted myself through the wall. Uncurled on the other side, within 6B Mason Drive, somewhere I'd never visited. Torch heavy in my hand. Rocks and broken plaster underfoot.

"I wish Lincoln was here," Dee said.

Her pale face through the hole, bleached by the torch I shone in her eyes.

"What?" I said. "What you mean?"

"This is like when we were at The Truck Graveyard," Dee said. "The three of us exploring. He'd be good here. With us. Wouldn't he? We're good at keeping secrets." Dee smiled. "Lincoln's your best friend," she said.

It wasn't a question. I answered it anyway. "Sure."

"Are boys allowed to have best friends?" she asked.

"I don't know," I said, a lump forming in my throat. "I really don't know."

Dee stepped back from the hole. Into silhouette. "Be careful."

I gripped the torch, lifted it high. The stink of mushrooms was strong in the basement of 6B Mason Drive. And there was something beneath that smell, too. Something sharp and eye-watering. Copper, perhaps. Citrus? Yes. Lemons.

"Whoa."

Growths had sprouted from the walls. They criss-crossed and joined, melded and split into arches I shuffled under, ducking my head. Shadows swirled, making me feel dizzy. I touched one of these evolutions to steady myself, only to find it wasn't as hard as expected. The material glowed, maybe even tensed under my palm, and seemed to make the interconnecting branches hum.

*Holy shit,* I thought. *It's alive.*

All around me, the growths glowed, as though by touching them I aggravated their minerals. I let go, hum fading. Hunger dulled awe. Had my guts grown teeth and started chewing again, opening holes in my innards like the hole between the two houses? I rubbed my stomach through the fabric of my shirt, wondering if *I* was going to glow as well, if light would shine through my fingers like a Care Bear belly in the cartoons Dee loved and I said I didn't love, but did. Because that was a girl's show. Because there were rules that had to be obeyed in the ecosystem. Only nothing stirred. No music from me.

I directed the torch at the staircase leading into the kitchen above. It was eerie how the room echoed the layout of our townhouse next door, each a mirror-image of the other. Except for a few crucial differences, of course. Like the spores that floated in the air over here, and how the walls were webbed in a knit-work of flesh vines. Yes. Flesh. Pale and clammy.

"Incredible," I said aloud, the word slipping out.

The nearest growth contracted as I brushed by it, tiny slits appearing in its surface, like a dozen tight cuts that whistled varying pitches. The chorus bled together to make the shape of a word.

*"Iiiinnnnnccccrrreeedddhhhhhiiibbbbbbbbblllllllleeeeee."*

This mimic—so like my voice, yet foreign—sent a chill through me. That shock was nothing compared to the way my body reacted to the sight of the creature emerging from the space under the stairs. How the hairs along my arms stood on end. Piss jetted down the inside of my thigh. Hunger flared again. The creature moved quick, gliding through flesh beams with grace. It landed in front of me with a thump, bones clattering beneath its skin as it rose. My arms raised in self-defence, light and dark in chaos as the torch swung. A flash of brightness in my eyes—only it wasn't from the bulb.

It came from the sun.

---

Sunlight seeps through the window and onto the bed where we lay together. Her touch is magnificent. She stares at me with jade eyes, my reflection in their darkest points. I raise a hand to cup her breast, tracing the curve of her neck to the lobe of her ear, her lips. They part and swallow my thumb. Jesus. She's a beauty. My thumb comes out wet.

Sleep would be easy. I can't do that. I need to get to work, and when I crawl off the mattress and back into my work clothes, I feel those jade eyes boring into me.

"When do you think you'll leave your wife?" she says.

And then I know the time has come.

---

Visions spored into twirling mist, re-revealing the creature from under the stairs. It had been with me all along, watching as Dee and I nervously chatted through its hole in the wall, as I explored what used to be a basement but was now its lair. I longed for the warmth of the vision again, painful as it had been. Dad's last day couldn't save me.

It was part-human, part-animal, a knot of beings wrung together like different coloured putty in a kindergarten class. Cat hair grew in places, grafts of skin in others, the chest a patchwork of boils over caved-in ribs. A long flaccid cock dangled between its legs.

Recognition *clunked* in my brain.

The creature resembled a character on one of the covers at

Top Video Universe, an illustration from a movie I'd never seen, but been obsessed by, which I'd held and memorised and sketched in our basement. There was no mistaking it. I'd laboured over the drawing, traced the original with my fingertips, imagined what it sounded like when it let loose its warnings. Daydreamed about the people it murdered and then ate.

The Slaughterer.

*I did this.*

*Me.*

It lowered its head, staring with feline eyes that surely couldn't see the way I saw the world, irises with no whites reflecting my mouth screaming. The torch revealed a hair-lip that divided its upper jaw from snout to mouth, cheeks puffing in a pained smile. Recognition hit me hard. The mouth. That hair-lip. Echoes of Brett Oldfield in the creature's mix.

"*Sweeeetttttt Jeeeesssuuusssss,*" it said in my father's voice, revealing teeth that grew in every direction. Its breath stunk of chemicals and paint and basement oils. The hurt those two words inflicted was almost beautiful, as if that pain were something I wanted. A distracting pinch. After all, there was so much of myself to hate. And I knew it. The creature knew it. That was why its look wasn't mean or threatening. It pitied me because it understood me.

"*Sweeeetttttt Jeeeesssuuusssss.*"

Something in me tore. I knew, then, those were my father's last words. He said them when the creature came for him.

Puzzle pieces came together. Dad must have come back to the house after being with the woman with the red hair.

(The rotting apple in our basement next door).

He came back for his lunch. Now, us, the rest of Dad's family, were left behind to survive what he hadn't. Maybe death was a blessing. Only the unlucky grieved.

Noise thundered overhead. And Dee screamed for our mother.

Mum and Aunt Kat were back.

The creature pushed me aside and sped to its hole in the wall, scuttling on hands and knees, dexterous as a dancer—only a dancer with a long, thrashing rat's tail swinging from its hide. I zoomed the torch in its direction, light swirling through this cathedral of dust and strange meat and shadows with too many teeth.

# TWO

I FLICK THE WASHING MACHINE ONTO ITS SIDE—NO LONGER
CARING ABOUT TRESPASSING UNSEEN AND UNHEARD.
I HAVE RECOVERED, RE-STRENGTHENED FROM MY LAST
CONSUMPTION, AND THE STAR OF THE MAN WHO HAD BEEN
IN THIS SPACE HAS BECOME A DEAD SUN OVERLOOKING THE
GALAXIES IN MY BELLY. IT TOOK A WHILE TO BE READY FOR
THIS, BUT READY I—WE—ARE.

THE GIRL-CHILD TRIES TO RUN AWAY FROM ME, RUN
UP THE STAIRS, TRAILING SHADOWS AND PUFFS OF STEAM
IT CANNOT SEE YET I CAN. HER CALLIGRAPHY. I READ AND
TONGUE IT. SWEET. SHE KNOWS I HAVE COME HERE TO EAT
HER, AND I AM ECSTATIC THAT SHE KNOWS.

A PUSH OF THESE ARMS, A COMPRESSION OF SPINE.
FLESH IS HEAVIER THAN BEFORE. MOVING FAST ISN'T EASY.
THAT IS HOW SHE GETS AWAY FROM MY REACH.

FIGURES EMERGE AT THE TOP OF THE STAIRS TO
GREET HER. THEIR STEAMS MINGLE AND SPELL FAMILY. THE
STAR BURNS FOR THEM, A SONAR SO STRONG IT WILL CAUSE
TSUNAMIS ELSEWHERE.

WE WILL HAVE THEM ALL.

"RUN, DEE!" I shouted, pushing myself through the gap separating the two townhouses. The torch slipped from my hand and hit the scratched-up concrete, blinking out in a stutter of glass. Screams filled our home. Three voices at once. All female.

All family.

Dust gouged at my eyes as I wriggled onto the floor, rolling to view the underside of the washing machine. Small black spiders scurried across my arms, muscles straining but pushing on. I climbed the stairs. Tripping. Getting up. Running. Toward the kitchen where the shrill noises were louder.

I stumbled again, shooting across the threshold, my feet knocking shards of wood splayed across the patterned linoleum. Our dining table—the place where we had eaten countless meals, despite us kids groaning how friends were allowed to chow down in front of the television—had been shattered, the cloth in shreds. Salt and sugar everywhere. Mum's gin bottle intact on the ground, dripping, dripping. I stepped over it, diving straight for the drawers beside the sink. Yanked it open. Snatched out a butcher knife. The blade was dull—they all were. No matter. The knife was just an extension of the real threat: *me*. The link I shared with the creature *had* to mean something. And hopefully, that something, whatever it was, could be weaponised.

A wave of adrenaline swept me through the kitchen, to the door to the living room. Knife slick in my hand. Gripped tight. Knuckles turned milky.

*Don't bail now. You can do this. You've got no choice, Spoons.*

Time slowed. In that elastic moment, I considered the crannies inside me where bravery grows, in the dark weak spots. Of course, bravery would spring from there. From your most vulnerable, and truest parts. Fragments that came together when nature required it most. When you had to either fly or fight. There was a sort of magic to that, I thought. Magic, which turned to strength. If you let it. Good magic. Good magic from good people.

Another scream shot from my lungs as I entered the living

room. A war cry, this time.

My eyes trailed Dee as she ran into Mum's room, not stopping to close the door behind her because our mother was still in the open, her face pitched with terror under the harsh ceiling light. Shadows pooled in her eyes, ran down her cheeks.

The creature, our front door at its back, had Aunt Kat in its arms. Aunt Kat, giver of chocolates and hugs that made you feel safe, who had always been the most loving. But also the slowest on her feet.

*This isn't fair.*

The Slaughterer heaved Aunt Kat into the air and thrashed her against the ceiling, the light fixture busting against her face. Sparks rained. Darkness, then, except for the television Dee had been gently snoring in front of before I woke her and insisted we go to the basement to try and make things right. Gravity dragged Aunt Kat to the carpet, the crash of her body making the room shake—vibrations that rippled up into my chest and throat, stifling my shock. Aunt Kat's silver hair fanned about her head, eye sockets and cheeks speared with slivers of glass. Mum and I screamed, our arms outstretched and pathetic, as The Slaughterer swiped its lion-like talons between Aunt Kat's legs, making her jolt, a single gag escaping her, a bubble of red popping in her mouth, and splitting her open from crotch to sternum. Clothes peeled away like skim off warmed milk. Blood painted The Slaughterer's face, so much like ink. It seemed indifferent, even bored. Aunt Kat's cane lay broken on the couch among the cushions. Not that she needed her cane. Not that she would ever need it again.

Mum shouted at me.

"Hide," I said through gritted teeth. "It's mine—"

The creature leapt on Aunt Kat again, painting the television red, filling the room with a crimson glow. Her head flopped in my direction, as though she could still see me. Aunt Kat danced on the ground as the monster ate her alive—just as Dad must have been consumed—tendons in her throat yanked tight so her mouth opened and closed, teeth clapping, a ventriloquist dummy in a kid's show, applauded by a sitcom audience on the screen.

Brightness filled my head.

———————————————————

"When do you think you'll leave your wife?" she says to me from where she lays on the bed.

(This question is fire.)

Her name is Ave, named after *Ave Maria*, or so she told me when we met, when I'd followed her to the bar after calling the woman I'd married on the payphone outside, telling her that I had to work late at the factory. Ave had been so easy to charm.

Snowy's got a trustworthy face. People say that about me all the time.

(The fire feels good. It was always going to end like this.)

This isn't one of my fantasies. It feels so strange—and electrifying—to have played this out in my imagination for so long only to have it coming true. On her mattress. On her good sheets. Ave's throat turns red under my grip. Eyes bulge, tears spill, veins pop-pop-pop. And it's me who is doing this to her. Me.

"Hear me!" I scream in her face. If only words were knives. But it was never going to be knives with her. It had to be with my hands. We wore rubbers when we fucked, but now there's nothing between us. More honest this way. This is the first time I've been truthful with her in our four-month affair. The game was worth it just to watch her shock when I pounced.

My smile to a scowl to a smile again.

She rakes at my clothes, trying to fight me off. The cunt can't even do that. Weak bitch. I choke her harder.

This is what I've always wanted, one of my many dreams. In the past, I curbed these urges by drawing in the books in my study, the ones I hid on the top shelf where the kids can't reach, scribbled cuts and spread legs and split nipples and bruised faces and mouths with the punched in teeth and chainsaws where the sun don't shine, all in the margins. My wife, THE WOMAN I SMILE AT, never goes into my study. She lets me be. Mostly. Pretending to love THE WOMAN I SMILE AT is getting harder. I think I killed Ave so I don't kill her.

The dream is dead. I'm awake now.

"HEAR ME!" I scream at the corpse.

She ain't hearing anything.

───── ── ─ ═ ── ── ─ ── ─ ── ─ ── ───── ─── ──── ── ─ ──

*No. Please, no.*

Dad hadn't come back to our house after the murder to pick up his lunch. He'd returned for an alibi. To make a phone call, perhaps. Something that would prove he'd been *here* and not *there.* Strolling out of the kitchen that last morning without the brown paper bag had been deliberate. This insight was a bashing. I'd overheard Mum calling our father a bastard on the phone to Aunt Kat. That had hurt at the time, but now I knew she was right. I knew that more than anyone. A lying, cheating, murdering bastard.

No wonder Mum and Aunt Kat had returned so soon.

Ave wouldn't have answered her door no matter how long they knocked, alfoil pinwheels spinning without their owner to admire them ever again. And what if the woman with the red hair *had* answered? Puppies chasing cars, that's all they were. Catch it and then what? *Stop thinking this way,* I told myself, somehow managing to grip the knife so tight it hurt. *Ave's in her room where Dad left her.* A splice of her: the face bruised from asphyxiation, tongue bulging, eyes rolled back but not all the way, crests of jade irises like upside down moons setting beneath eyelid horizons. Dad was in the monster, and the monster was in me. Consumed within the consumed and ready to consume again. That this hunger might never end terrified me.

The Slaughterer bellowed. Cracks formed in the plaster walls as if in response. Oxygen seemed to thin, and I struggled to breathe again. There weren't just cracks now, but blisters like those that formed upstairs when the posters came alive.

"NO!" I screamed at the monster and what it did, at my father.

It didn't stop, of course. It was here for a purpose, a mission that hadn't been achieved. Yet.

My mother and I watched Aunt Kat's blood peel off the walls, floor, ceiling, and television, drawn through the air as if by a magnet—and the magnet was *it*, the creature. Particles swirled into helixes, defying gravity, funnelling into that hair-lipped mouth. Gulp. It drank Aunt Kat's blood, not a drop wasted. The Slaughterer's hands touched its chest, talons curling into the flesh. It yanked itself open, batwing ribcages swinging like a meat coat to expose an enormous sideways throat, a second mouth with flytrap teeth. Even in the dim light, I saw the hole in the creature's core, and how that hole had depth that shouldn't (couldn't) be there (but was), a kind of optical illusion, a funnel into nothingness. These barbed wings swooped low and snatched Aunt Kat whole, snapping her in two, bones spearing through the gore, ballooning fat and shit-filled intestines. Crunch. The Slaughterer heaved itself upright again, ribcages drawing together, and I felt the pain in my stomach—that cancerous need for food—soften. Another gulp. A satisfying gulp. The woman with the silver hair who had come to this house to help her family when they needed help most was gone.

Devoured.

Mum—face pale as the sheets she'd hung in the yard—took the creature's feeding as an opportunity to run for her bedroom where Dee was howling. She waved at me to escape out back as she slipped through the door, clipping her shoulder on the architrave, perhaps the final sluggishness of the gin she'd downed. I couldn't run. No. The Slaughterer wasn't distracted any more. I'd seen how fast it moved. Satisfied, for now, it opened its sad eyes to glare into me, seeking affirmation, its look asking if I was happy with what happened here tonight.

*Because I did this for you, Heath.*
*And not for the first time, either.*

---

I step to the door leading into the basement in our house, my work boots scuffing the linoleum I'd laid years before. This isn't my home any more. To some degree, I hadn't existed within these walls for years. The outline of someone other people think I am walked these corridors and explored these rooms.

Weird sounds coming from downstairs break my pins-and-needles thoughts.

One hand grips the lunch bag THE WOMAN I SMILE AT prepared that morning, the other touching the handle to the basement door. Soft light filters from below. Something shifts at the bottom of the stairs. Twin glimmers. Eyes. Cat-like eyes. For a moment, I think they belong to Ave, as if she isn't dead and climbed her way back to me, fingernails snapping when she dragged herself across the hot road between her place and mine.

"Who the fuck is down there?"

Only no, it's not her looking up at me. Her red hair isn't on display, her red face after I was done with her. This thing is bald. And it is huge.

It rushes at me. Spilling over itself, using the walls to thrust itself up the staircase.

A huge mouth opens sideways.

"Sweet Jesus!" I manage to cry, the two words making its black eyes glimmer.

It isn't a man, but a monster, something from one of the movies Heath can't get enough of. Jaws snap my face. There's no time to move or escape—and even if there had been, I'm not sure I would have anyway. Maybe this is meant to be. The creature will take me to whatever comes next. Maybe in whatever comes next, I'm seen, I'm heard.

Pain ignites. Surprise. Death hurts. I am ground to jelly. A thousand needles and nails shred me open. Pressure forces me down, up, sideways, thrashed this way and that. I'm stupid in the face of this power. It's killing me. I'm dying.

Fear.

Everything slides to black as I'm swallowed. It has taken my eyes. I feel it drinking me dry, my innards funnelled out. A million parts of me snap, implode, explode, turns inward, flips outwards. Nerves fire. There is no mercy in the monster.

I used to be a man. I used to be THE PERSON WHO SMILED at THE WOMAN I SMILE AT. Now I'm something new. I am a seed. I feel myself being planted somewhere else. Whatever story I owned ends now. Eyeless, my sight closes on one world, and in this dark every question is answered. The seed takes root.

There are no gods, only teeth.

---

Mum emerged from her bedroom, something shiny gripped in both hands. Her warrior's yell dragged me back to reality. She launched at the creature from where it swayed in the middle of our living room, as though the weight of all that aunty meat had thrown it off kilter. Its stubby legs thudded the carpet, flipping the coffee table and sending the plates Dee and I had eaten off through the air.

She attacked from behind.

Pride for Mum beamed through me.

I saw her as she was, but also as the young woman in the photograph tucked into the pocket of my shorts from where I'd stowed it earlier in the day, after I hurt Brett. The lithe girl who strengthened me, impossibly young. Who did that adult version see when she looked in the mirror? Did she see the things time took from her? Could she name them? Or do you just sense the absence when you're older? Maybe she sees what I see in her. Cleverness. Regret. A refusal to take things lying down. And a dash of suspicion—though she had good reason to be suspicious. Mum was in a mystery whether she wanted to be or not. We all were. And I was convinced that if we survived this, when she learned the truth about the man she'd married, the woman in the mirror would vanish, just as the girl in the photograph in my pocket no longer existed. Suspicion turned to steel. Nobody would ever be let in again.

*Do it, Mum. Get him.*

She brought one of the two iron shots she kept in her room down on the creature's scalp. A splitting fruit sound clapped off the walls, a sound I felt in my bones.

The Slaughterer hit the carpet, neck twisting at an unnatural angle—not that there was anything natural about it to begin with. It gagged, and in my father's voice again, said, "*Swwwwweeeetttt Jeeeesssuuuussss*". If I heard it, then so did Mum. Empty-handed, she backed against Dee in the architrave, where she stood cupping the final shot, shoulders pinched under the weight. Dee's eyes widened. She watched the creature stumble, curtains swirling, mementos tipping off the shelves, as it lumbered to the front door, its energy (its magic) reshaping the air, paint peeling off the walls, lamps ripped from power sockets. Moonlight through the window lit its bloodied face. It raised a taloned hand to the door for balance, wincing.

Mum and Dee braved a run in my direction.

Seven yards of carpet lay between us. The last of my family were field mice in hawk territory. Tears peeled from their faces as they ran. Mum reached out to me, gripped my shirt and hefted me off my feet, trying to force me back into the kitchen.

I slipped, almost bringing them both down with me. Held true. Just. But I lost my grip on the knife, watched it sail away.

The (my) creature spun and rose to its full stature again, floorboards yanked up around it, shredding the carpet. Dust flying. Spores. Photos from the walls whirled like startled bats in a cave. Electricity sparked in sockets, flashes revealing The Slaughterer's patchwork hide, its now erect cock, and worse, the way its scalp was *consuming* Mum's iron shot, sucking it into its skull, breaking it down.

"Heath!" Mum screamed. "GO."

She dragged me through the kitchen to the door to the yard as the creature lumbered after us, its huge arms shuttling it into action. *"Sweeeetttt Jeeesssuuusss,"* it moaned again. *"Sweeeeeeeettttttttttttt Jeeeesssussssssssssssssssssssssss!"*

In the chaos of it all, I caught a whiff of my mother's perfume beneath the booze, the essence of her. That sweetness was benign and loving, even if there had been times in my life when I hadn't understood that love. I regretted knocking back every invitation to sit with her, the kisses I dodged because—*jeeze*—I was 'too old' for that kind of thing.

The Slaughterer moved with a feline quality, tail whipping. As in the living room, the composition of the kitchen altered, architecture warping like wax under flame. Glass detonated from the windows. The tap by the sink wrenched sideways to spray water over us as my sister forced the screen door open.

My creature outstretched its arm.

Just as it appeared on the VHS cover at Top Video Universe.

We made it outside. Wind sent the sheets and linen into riot. Leaves slapped our faces as we tried to run, tripping over those cotton skins instead. Black night. White fabric. Black. White. Black. White. Here. There. Everywhere.

"Mum!" Dee yelled.

"Over here—"

My mother's grip slipped from mine. I lost them both in the rush.

Linen looped my ankles, dragging me to the ground where I'd buried the mixtape. Dirt plumed into my mouth. Earth shuddered. That's how I knew it was closing in on us. My hand flailed in the dark. Peekaboo moon. Gripped dried grass to tug myself upright.

Something snatched me by the collar. I collided with my mother. "Your sister," she said. "W-where's your sister?"

*"Sweeeeetttttttt Jeeeessssuuussssssss!"*

Nothing made sense. Up turned down. Right turned wrong. All I could do was shout Dee's name. Again and again.

Mum drew me through whipping linen towards the dead lemon tree. My foot stubbed something hard, pain rocketing up my leg. I didn't get a chance to see what I'd almost gone head-over-arse on because Mum had already swooped to snatch it up. Moonlight caught the glimmer of its polished surface.

The last iron shot.

Gasping, we passed through the remaining sheets across the clothesline as fence palings shook free of their nails to soar through the sky. The gate clattered against its hinge in the corner. Beyond, trashcans overturned.

"That way," Mum told me, pointing. "Now."

"I *need* to be here," I said, panting. "This thing is mine."

"What?"

"It—"

My sister's shriek cut the night. Mum raised the shot, primed to attack. Clothes wafted on her wiry frame, shoulders squared, legs spread.

*"Come at me,"* Mum yelled.

The sheets on the line whipped, rising and falling, movement on the other side.

She stepped away from me.

Mum didn't need to say she loved me. I know she did. But looking back, I wish she had. One last time. I wish she'd told me she didn't know who Dad was when we all weren't around, though I'm sure she didn't. I wish my mother said all the things I needed to hear for me to be whole again, someday.

The Slaughterer split the sheets, so casual. It glanced around like those men re-emerging from the sectioned-off area at Top Video Universe, with their dirty thoughts and dirty movies. A shoulder emerged next. But Mum—

*(THE WOMAN I SMILE AT)*

—held her ground. The creature's face had changed. Or maybe I'd misread it the first time, down in the basement of 6B Mason Drive. I don't know. I wish I did, believe me. If I'd been wrong once, then I could be incorrect again. Who knows, maybe I'm remembering all this wrong. Maybe none of this happened. Maybe I'm not alone. Then again, I know better. Scars are a one-way street.

Its eyes were humanoid now, and familiar. Mum had seen them peering at her from her breast, watched them shy from the sun on rare holidays we indulged in as a family, had watched them widen with joy at films on the television.

The eyes were mine.

Mum's confidence wavered as The Slaughterer with my face heaved Dee above the clothesline. The little girl in the overalls punched as best she could, efforts that amounted to nothing. It ripped her face open, gushing blood and gurgling yelps.

"LET GO OF MY BABY!"

Clouds swirled over the moon.

*"Sweeeeeeeetttttt—"* began Dad's voice in the monster's mouth. *"Jesus,"* finished my voice in the monster's mouth.

A quiet hush fell over the yard. Wind dropped every sheet and leaf in straight lines. Mum kept her armed hand raised, swivelling to me instead. Me, her son. Moon shadow swiped her face of its fight. What re-emerged was an emptiness that was a mask. She overfilled with purpose, knew what she was doing. Mum had a plan. That was why she stepped in *my* direction, not at the creature.

She raised the heavy, iron shot. Her knowing eyes twinkled.

Behind Mum, over her shoulder, I saw my creature twist Dee's head from her shoulders. Did every star blink out? Just for a moment? I hoped my mother didn't hear rain that wasn't there, didn't see or feel its warmth as part of what she gave this world died. Spiflicated. Spiflicated beyond repair. You didn't come back from something like that. Never. All the nevers in the Milky Way.

"Mum," I said, panic rising. "NO—"

She ran at me. "It'll work. Trust me! I'm *sorry!*"

(THE WOMAN I SMILE AT) swung the shot, bringing it down on my face.

# ONE

Thunder rumbled through the dark, even though there was no lightning. The sound was a release. And in that millisecond before unconsciousness stole me away, I stupidly thought:

*It's over.*

# ZERO

There are things I remember about what happened next, and things I don't, a precedent beginning that night and continuing to this day. Calling it a selective self-defence mechanism would be nice, but then again, that wouldn't be true. Damage was done.

Memory shards.

The dead lemon tree I woke under after Mum knocked me out in the hope it would, in turn, incapacitate the creature I was linked to. Bark splashed in blue and red light. Stars as the clouds slid away. The sensation of being pulled at, lifted. The room that wasn't a room, but the back of an ambulance, and how it rocked. A needle in the crook of my arm. Men and women. Questions. Nurses with bandages. Louis Demeeter in his police uniform telling me it was okay to cry, and him bringing me the photograph of my mother that emergency staff found in the shorts I'd been wearing. More questions. The mental health ward I was admitted to months later and the art classes they tried to get me to engage in, even going to the extent of putting the pencil in my hand. Me asking doctors if Lincoln or even Tina could visit me. And being told soon, Heath. Soon.

They never did come, though.

Being dropped into foster care in Newcastle and then in Sydney, some of those well-intentioned pretend mothers and pretend fathers being nice to me, some of them not so nice, all trying to feed and keep me in school. The boss who fired from a job packing shelves because I stole alcohol.

Memories of running away. Memories of the police dragging me back. Memories of running away again.

Turning seventeen with a cake and everything, and how my foster parents broke down when I thanked them for putting up with me, when I told them I was gay. They gifted me an old bicycle, a Schwinn, told me they knew I'd get there, given time. I'm not allowed to drive. The vision in my right eye is almost non-existent, and I'm prone to seizures.

Memories of running away for good after my monster found me.

I saw it with my good eye, peering at me from inside a curb drain. Talon fingers curling over the concrete, reaching for me, stinking of the sewer and citrus. Its tongue reaching out to taste my thoughts.

*"Brought you chocolate,"* it said in Aunt Kat's voice. *"Sweeeeeettttttt."*

Hitting the road on my bike. A journey marked in leg cramps not *Simpsons* episodes. Sleeping in places I shouldn't. The men I fucked in trade for anything that made the hurt bearable. Track marks where I used to pinch. Two years with no home. Turning street mean when I had to. Eating leftovers in alleys and stealing to stay alive. Stopping and just being *still* did me no good—that only gifted my monster, the shadow with too many teeth, valuable catch-up time. And somewhere along the line, I decided to go back to Townsend Heights. To some degree, I always knew it would go that way.

Only now I'm here, I don't know what to do. Another puppy chasing another car.

The $250 Marge at The Salvation Army gave me has almost run out. I'll be broke after tonight's accommodation at the Big Rex Inn on Hunter Street. It's fitting in a way that I will kick off the first day of the year 2000 back at square one, considering everyone's Y2K panic. I don't regret blowing the money on a few nights of cheap, bed-buggy accommodation. That Sealy Posturepedic lived up to its advertised hype, and I'm pretty sure I brought the bugs with me.

I avoided Mason Drive because I remember hearing that the council tore the townhouses down years ago, and yesterday, glutton for punishment, I went to the Leoungs' house instead. The thing with being shafted into the child protection system is that all your prior relationships vanish overnight, and especially if your departure is wrapped up in a criminal investigation. I longed to see my old friend one more time.

The Leoungs no longer lived there, and the woman who answered the door wept when I asked after them. She gave me a hard once-over first, staring at my scuffed boots, my ripped jeans, the stains on my shirt. And the scars on my face, of course. The scars that define me.

Because I'm the guy who has lived, see.

"What did you say your name was again?" she asked. I answered truthfully. I hadn't said my real name aloud since running away two years ago. "Oh, Heath," she said. "Mister Leoung and his daughter moved away after his wife and son were killed in a car accident."

I'm going to pretend Lincoln never existed, that I never gave his sister that mixtape. They're in The Great Never Was. Only they're not alone over there. Mum, my sister, and Aunt Kat are there, too. I believe we linger in this universe for as long as we're remembered. Sometimes the responsibility of having all those souls living on in me is too much to take.

The memory of Ave Casey slips through.

Nobody was sentenced for her murder. How could there be? My father was never found.

Afterwards, I rode my Schwinn around town in the dark, not wanting to be seen or recognised. Houses slithered by. They were each someone's face, windows for eyes and doors for mouths, all mute. Wheels *tick, tick, tick, ticked*. Streetlamps illuminated cracks in the sidewalk. I avoided them for fear of falling and breaking my grandmother's back. Dee occupied my mind. We were children who believed in magic because believing in magic was part of what made us children. Only with age, crystals turned to coal.

St Joseph's still stood, and maybe some of the same ignorant teachers taught there. Brett Oldfield's house hadn't changed, either. It was quieter, at least. There were shoes strung over powerlines by their laces out front, which you didn't have to be streetwise to know signalled drug dealers on-site. Maybe I'm not shocked to learn that's how things ended up for a family like that. You had to survive somehow.

There was a VCR under the television in my room at the Big Red Inn, and a few tapes at reception for guests to borrow. To my surprise, one of the films in the collection was *The Slaughterer*. I turned the clamshell over in my hands. The price sticker covered half of the monster's outstretched hand. In the bottom right-hand corner, almost scraped away, evidence of the video's prior life remained:

### PROPERTY OF TOP VIDEO UNIVERSE.

Words can't describe how quickly anxiety turned to sadness. Shaking, I slid the cassette into the machine in my room.

It clattered and clunked. Tracking kicked into overdrive as the VCR tried to scrub dirt off the heads. I sat through trailers with a beer I couldn't afford wedged between my legs, three dollars' worth of shakes from the Magic Fingers function mustering a little hocus pocus. Eighty-three minutes (including credits) of cheap carnage ensued, my attention wavering. Women screamed on cue, bled as they were supposed to bleed. I caught a glimpse of a zipper up The Slaughterer's back during the final chase, and sighed.

All the lamps are off in my room at the Inn. Fireworks explode in the lot across the road, skittering pink and blue light through the blinds. It's loud on the street with people partying, ready to welcome in the year 2000. Hoots. Breaking glass. I volley between asleep and awake. Sometimes, I bolt upright, thinking Mum and Dee are in the room with me, that I've heard the tap of Aunt Kat's cane.

The digital clock on the bedside table reads 11:51pm.

*Scratch-scratch. Scratch-scratch.*

I sit up again, shirtless and doused in sweat. The air conditioner isn't working. My boxer shorts stick to my legs as I swing around, feet landing on the tacky carpet. The chattering of my teeth is loud in this room in the town I grew up in, back when I was the son of a murderer, someone's big brother and nephew, someone's best friend, a student, the bully's target, the boy the girl didn't want and that was okay in the end.

*Scratch-scratch. Scratch-scratch. Scratch-scratch-scratch.*

Something hollows out in the pit of me, stillness I don't want to admit is contentedness. I'm so tired of running.

*Scratch. Scratch-scratch.*

Reconciled, I cross the room, flip the lock, and open the door. Paint flakes off the plywood walls, lilting like seedlings. A Bible on the small reading table to my right curls in on itself and bubbles like gum, popping, dripping to the floor. Even the solidity of the handle shifts under my grip, steel turning to foam.

The door creaks wide, revealing the numbers 248 beneath the peephole I didn't bother to peep through because I knew who was out there. Warm, syrupy air flows over my face.

It stands in the architrave, which warps in front of me, growths spindling outwards and upwards, each branch decorated with little slits that wink. Light stutters from the fireworks, lending a blue and pink glow to its face, its shoulder, its chest and hips like dunes at midnight. It smells like shit and lemons and sweetness. Terror should send me running. But there's only numbness now. Another sliver of memory, an old copy of *SWANKSTERS* in The Truck Graveyard and how it made me feel, the door it opened.

Clayton McManus speaks in my voice.

*"Muuuummmm,"* it says.

Something blooms in my head and takes hold. Accepting it feels good. There is no fear. I step aside to let my monster in. Hinges squeak behind it, and then darkness again. Except for the glow through the window, the digital clock as it clicks to midnight, at which point, silence consumes everything. Beat (going). There is no bar fridge drone any more. Beat (going). The clock is dead. Beat (gone). Even the partiers have stilled outside—though not for long. Quiet shock gives way to screams that fill the night, in the lot and across town, maybe further. Maybe everywhere in the world. Guests rush from their rooms, yelling for loved ones who cry and shout, "What's happening? No, my God, no!" But me? I'm not alone. We step close to the glass, my monster and I, close enough to hear how our breaths have syncopated. Together, we draw back the curtain to watch planes fall from the sky, and for the first time in a long time, WE THINK THINGS MIGHT BE OKAY.

## ACKNOWLEDGEMENTS

I'd like to take this opportunity to briefly thank the following people.

Alpha Cheng for the support, though he insists he didn't do much, when in reality, support is everything. The Black T-Shirt bois for being the bois—especially Scott Cole for your wizardry. Katie Taylor for your editorial eye. John Boden for the generosity. Kaaron Warren and J. Ashley-Smith for the laughs and cats and dinners. Thon for the incredible art. And the reader for coming back.

The reader always.

# ABOUT THE AUTHOR

Author, artist, and filmmaker, Aaron Dries was born and raised in New South Wales, Australia. His novels include *House of Sighs*, *The Fallen Boys*, *A Place for Sinners*, and *Where the Dead Go to Die*, which he co-wrote with Mark Allan Gunnells. His first collection of short stories, *Cut to Care*, will be published in 2022. Aaron is also a co-host of the popular podcast, *Let the Cat In*.

Feel free to drop him a line at:
aarondries.com
Twitter @AaronDries
TikTok @aarondries_writer
Or, on Instagram at aarondries

BE KIND, REWIND

Made in the USA
Middletown, DE
07 September 2022

73403031R00085